SPEAK TO ME

KYLIE QUILLINAN

First published in Australia in 2022.

ABN 34 112 708 734

kyliequillinan.com

A catalogue record for this book is available from the National Library of Australia.

Ebook ISBN: 9780645377132

Paperback ISBN: 9780645377149

Large print ISBN: 9780645377156

Hardback ISBN: 9780645377163

Audiobook ISBN: 9781922852540

This is a work of fiction. Any similarity between the characters and situations within its pages and places or persons, living or dead, is unintentional and coincidental.

Cover art by Moorbooks Design. Editing by Eliza Dee.

This work uses Australian spelling and grammar.

LP17012025

CHAPTER
ONE

The day the spirits first spoke to me started like any other Monday. I woke twenty minutes after my alarm should have gone off. No time for breakfast. Quick shower, a dash of lipstick and a ponytail. Grabbed my battered old handbag.

As I unlocked the front door, a noise made me pause. Someone talking, a child. Not a very young one though. Teenaged, maybe. But I lived alone and unless a child had somehow snuck into the house while I slept, which would seem impossible considering the locked door, the logical conclusion was that I was hearing things.

I needed a holiday, that was all. I hadn't taken a proper break in years and had even been called into work on Christmas Day. It wasn't like it disrupted my plans since I had only intended to microwave a frozen meal and eat in front of the television. I didn't have anyone to celebrate with, anyway. No friends to speak of and I hadn't spoken to my parents in nine years. Not since my brother died.

They blamed me for his death. Nobody ever said it out loud, but I knew. He had tried to contact me the day he died. Left a voicemail saying he needed to talk to me urgently. I listened to the message on my lunch break. I heard the anguish in his voice, but I had too much to do that afternoon and figured I'd call him when I got home, when my boss wouldn't be looking over my shoulder, and I would have the head space to deal with whatever his problem was. But I ended up stuck at work until late and by the time I got home, I was too tired to bother. He was already dead by then, not that anyone realised for three days. In all that time, I still never got around to returning his call.

The walk to the train station was as unpleasant as usual. I lived on a busy road and by the time I left the house each morning, exhaust fumes and car horns already filled the air. What wouldn't I give to move out to the country somewhere? Be surrounded by grass and trees and cows. I inhaled deeply, pretending I breathed in clean, country air, and choked on the fumes belching from a passing truck. I made it to the station just as the train pulled in. It was a thirty-minute ride, then a two-block walk to the office.

I worked as an administrative officer for a small accounting firm. Once upon a time, we were called secretaries, but apparently that's not politically correct these days. I don't mind my job. Not really. It's mindless, and some days it's soul-sucking, but I wasn't the sort who grew up knowing what they wanted to do with the rest of their lives and I don't like to dwell on might-have-beens. So I go to work, do my job, and go home again.

"Morning, Mac," I called as I passed my boss's office. He grunted and waved, but didn't look up from his computer. Mac — Mackenzie McKenzie — was one of those unfortunate people whose parents really didn't think when they chose their baby's name. He usually wasn't very communicative, except when he wanted me to do something.

I unlocked my computer, opened my emails, and got to work. At ten o'clock, I went to the lunchroom to make a coffee. I have one coffee a day at precisely ten a.m. It's a small vice, but I don't have many of them. I don't drink, don't smoke, and I've never taken an illegal drug. I don't even take painkillers. So I let myself have a coffee a day and try not to think about whether that counts as an addiction. I always have two shortbread biscuits with my coffee. I guess that's another vice.

I sat down with a sigh, thankful the break room was empty. Monday mornings were always manic. Mac worked right through the weekend, so I came in to two days' worth of emails, mostly about letters he wanted me to type. Although he was quite proficient with email and could obviously type to some extent, he insisted on handwriting letters when I wasn't around to dictate them to. Then he scanned them and emailed them to me. Like I said, it's a job. It pays my mortgage.

Peggy walked in just as I finished my coffee. She was blond, pretty and vacuous. Mac had hired her less than six months ago and I was never quite sure what she did other than make another cup of coffee every half an hour. I hurried back to my desk, thankful to get away before being forced to make small talk with her.

The rest of the day was uneventful. Mac didn't have much for me to do that afternoon, so I busied myself with some neglected filing. It wasn't really one of my duties, but I can't stand sitting around doing nothing. I popped into Mac's office mid-afternoon to check whether he had anything else for me. He got a funny look on his face, shook his head, and busied himself with tapping away on his keyboard. More evidence he could really type.

When five o'clock arrived, I did a final check of my emails in case Mac had sent through any last-minute tasks. For once he hadn't, and it looked like I was actually going to leave work on time. I had just retrieved my handbag from the filing cabinet beside my desk when Mac appeared in the doorway of my office.

"Dorothy, could I see you for a moment before you leave?"

"Sure, Mac, what's the problem?"

His forehead wrinkled and he looked at his shoes.

"Let's talk in my office, hey?"

I tried to conceal my sigh as I set my handbag on my desk and followed him down the hallway. It drove me crazy that he would leave me sitting around half the day, then load a bunch of tasks on me just as I was about to leave. It seemed today was no different after all.

We reached Mac's office and he stood aside to let me enter the room first — an unusual courtesy from him — then closed the door. That probably should have told me to be worried, but my only thought was that the matter must be confidential.

"Dorothy, this is somewhat of an awkward thing we need to discuss." Mac's chair squeaked as he sat. He cleared his throat and stood up again, then positioned himself by the window, one hand tapping on the sill.

I waited, puzzled by his behaviour. Should I have brought a pen and notepad? Maybe he intended to dictate something for me to type but wanted to impress on me its importance first.

"Dorothy, I'm afraid we lost two of our biggest clients over the weekend. FBA has decided to hire their own in-house accountants and Jacobs Industries has taken their business to another accounting firm."

"That's terrible." I started to get a sneaking suspicion about the reason for his nervousness.

"As you know, those two clients alone comprised almost forty percent of our work."

I waited silently. I didn't intend to make this easier for him.

He cleared his throat again and stared out the window.

"Dorothy, I'm afraid we're going to have to let you go."

Now that he had actually said it, my mind went blank.

"Of course, you'll receive a redundancy package and I'm happy to write you a reference."

"Of course," I echoed, wishing I could think of a suitably crushing comment. Perhaps I wouldn't walk out feeling like such a loser if I could think of just the right thing to say, but my mind was blank.

Mac cleared his throat again and looked longingly out the window.

"Well," he said. "I should let you go. I mean, I should let you clear out your desk, that sort of stuff. Just forward me anything you haven't finished yet and—"

He stopped, perhaps catching himself before he said he'd get someone else to do it. Maybe Peggy would have to become something more than just office decoration.

"Yes, of course. I'll just get my things."

I rose, still feeling like I should say something meaningful. I should tell him how much it hurt that he had chosen me — a hard worker who had been with him from the start — rather than the waste of space that called herself Peggy.

Then I heard a voice in my ear. It sounded as if the speaker stood real close to me, but of course there was nobody in the room other than Mac and me.

"You should wish him well with his love child," the voice said.

I had no idea what that meant. Mac was one of the most straight-laced people I knew. He had been married for almost thirty years and I'd never heard even a whiff of office gossip about an affair.

"Don't let me keep you, Dorothy." Mac's face showed his discomfort and it was clear he wanted me gone as quickly as possible.

I went to the door and set my hand on the knob.

"You heard me, didn't you?" the voice said. "Why now, of all times? But anyway, are you really going to leave without saying anything? You'll regret it forever if you do. Go on, wish him well with the baby. I'm sure he'll appreciate it. After all, he checks his stocks every hour, then emails his financial advisor. He was trying to come up with the money to retire in less than five years, but now his mistress is having a baby and his retirement plans are in limbo. He's desperate to figure out how to pay for this baby without his wife finding out."

I coughed to cover the sudden laugh that threatened to burst out of me. Was there any chance the voice might be right? At that point, I wasn't wondering who the speaker was, or why he was invisible, only whether he told the truth. He was right. I would regret it if I didn't say something. Finally, I turned back to Mac, who was again staring fixedly out of the window.

"I wish you all the best, Mac." He turned back to me, his face surprised at the sincerity in my voice. "I hope everything goes well with the birth."

I left before I laughed, but not so quickly that I missed seeing his face turn tomato red.

There wasn't much to pack up in my office. Just my coffee cup and a small framed photo of my brother. I stashed them in my handbag, then deleted all my emails. I'd be damned if I was going to help anyone pick up the pieces after I left.

I had worked for Mac for ten years and yet it took less than ten minutes to prepare to leave. The front door shut behind me with an obnoxious squeak and I tried to feel good about walking out for the last time. I hadn't even thought to ask how much the redundancy package would be. Perhaps I should have tried to negotiate. I pushed the thought away. It was over and done with. No point going back to argue now.

"That was a pretty crappy way to let you go," the voice said as I set off at a brisk walk.

I ignored it. There would be time later to wonder whether I was losing my mind. For now, I wanted to get home before I fell apart. It had been just Mac and me originally, back when he first started the business. It had grown since then and a lot of staff had come and gone. Yet after everything, I was still there. I would have thought that counted for something. That if he had to let someone go, it wouldn't be me. But apparently loyalty and hard work mean nothing. I sniffed and blinked away a tear. I wouldn't let myself cry until I got home.

"He was horrified when you mentioned the baby." My invisible companion sounded like he smiled.

I didn't smile back and I didn't respond. The voice fell silent, leaving me with only my thoughts for company on the ride home.

CHAPTER
TWO

The house was quiet and empty when I arrived. There was nobody to greet me. Nobody to ask about my day. Nobody to see that I tossed my handbag onto the kitchen counter, dropped onto a bar stool, and burst into tears.

I let myself cry for exactly three minutes, then I wiped the tears away. No point wallowing in self pity, and my stomach was rumbling. Clearly, I was not the sort of person who lost their appetite in traumatic circumstances.

I opened the freezer and pulled out the first package I grabbed. According to the picture on the box, it was a thick piece of roast pork with vegetables and gravy. Inside was a thin, beige slice of something that might once have been meat, a quarter of a potato, half a carrot and eight shrivelled peas. The congealed grey lump was probably the advertised gravy. I sighed and tossed it in the microwave. Money would be tight until I found a new job and I couldn't afford to throw out good food. At least the freezer was well stocked.

I probably couldn't afford to waste good wine either, so I took a bottle of white from the wine rack on the counter. I didn't really drink, but I always kept a few bottles around in case of unexpected dinner guests. Not that guests ever happened, unexpected or otherwise. Those same bottles had been there for years. I didn't even know whether they were still drinkable. I tossed the white into the freezer and opened a bottle of red. No point wasting time while I waited for the wine to chill. I was going to get myself horribly drunk, so I didn't have to think about what had happened.

I leaned against the counter as I gulped down the first glass. Like the rest of the house, the kitchen had seen better days. The orange laminate counter peeled at the edges. Most of the cupboard doors were missing handles. The scratched wooden floor desperately needed a sand and polish. People said the second glass of red wine was always better than the first. I hadn't made it that far before, but I was well onto number two by the time the microwave beeped to indicate my meal was ready. It was true. Red wine did taste better on the second glass.

As I took my meal into the lounge room, I was already a little unsteady on my feet. I ate sitting on the battered couch as I flicked through the television channels, looking for something at least mildly interesting to watch. My meal didn't smell particularly edible, but it tasted slightly better than it looked.

"Lean times coming up, Dorothy," I muttered. "There might come the day yet when you'll be thankful for a crappy microwaved meal. Eat up and be grateful for what you've got."

Later, I couldn't remember what I had watched that night. I finished the bottle of red and stumbled off to retrieve the white from the freezer. My head was swimming pretty good by then. If I had any sense, I would have stopped there, but I was determined to get myself mind-numbingly drunk. I got halfway through the bottle of white before I had to run off to the bathroom to throw up. Maybe mind-numbingly drunk wasn't such a good idea.

As I lay in bed with my head spinning, the voice returned. Only this time, the invisible speaker brought a couple of friends.

"Do you think she'll be all right?" A young, female voice. Maybe the one I heard laughing before I left this morning.

"She'll be fine. She just needs to sleep it off." My invisible friend from Mac's office.

"I don't mean that." The female voice again. "I mean her job. What will she do now?"

"Don't you worry about it, Lis." Another female. Older than either of the others and with an authoritative, capable voice. "Dorothy's a practical sort. She'll figure something out. Why don't we leave her to sleep?"

"I might just stay here 'n keep an eye on her." Another male. Possibly the oldest of the group. "Just 'n case."

I fell into an uneasy sleep where the world spun and Mac kept asking me for advice on childbirth. I felt pretty sorry for myself when I woke the next morning. My head throbbed and my mouth was a strange combination of furry and metallic. This must be my first hangover.

I sat at the kitchen counter nursing a very large mug of chamomile tea and wishing it was coffee. I was thirty-five-years-old and I had never been fired before. Tomorrow I would pull myself together, but today I would watch daytime television and feel sorry for myself. Maybe I would even tackle another bottle of wine.

I couldn't remember ever sitting at home on a Tuesday before. Daytime television was even worse than I had heard and by mid-afternoon I was prowling the house, wishing I had someone to talk to. Maybe not here in the house with me, but someone I could ring. There was nobody who would care that I'd been fired. In a moment of weakness, I thought about ringing my mother before sanity washed over me. I had cut my parents out of my life for a reason and the fact that I'd just lost my job didn't change that.

There weren't any friends I could call either. I'd never really had close friends. Back in high school, there was always a shy nerd who didn't mind having someone to sit with in the library during lunch, but it was different once you left school. Nobody needed a friend who wanted to sit quietly in a place that discouraged talking. People wanted friends who were exciting and did stuff. I almost wished the imaginary voices would talk to me again, even though it probably indicated I was losing my mind.

Around six p.m. I started cooking some dinner. Nothing interesting, just a pan fried chicken breast with some beans. No butter for the beans. If I was going to look for a new job, it wouldn't hurt to lose a little weight. I had never thought of myself as fat, but I was certainly well-padded around the middle. The chicken sizzled in the pan and when I turned it over, the underside was nicely browned and crispy. I'm not much of a cook, but it actually smelled pretty tasty. Better than that frozen rubbish from last night anyway.

I ate on the couch in front of the television as usual. Tomorrow I would start looking for a new job, and maybe there would be opportunities to make friends. If not, I would have to find some other way to meet people. I couldn't go on like this. I didn't mind being on my own — I was too old for romance and all that nonsense anyway — but some friends would be nice.

THREE

On Wednesday morning, I booted up my ancient laptop and opened the file that contained my CV. But there wasn't anything much to update. I hadn't done any training or development in all the years I worked for Mac. I had asked to do some course or other a few times in the early years, but he always said he couldn't spare me and eventually I stopped asking. At least it made the job of updating my CV easy. I added the date I finished working for him and that was it. I closed the file, opened a web browser, and started searching for job vacancies.

An hour later, I was trying not to cry. I had thought this would be a chance to do something different. Learn a new job. Upskill myself. But every position that looked even mildly interesting required qualifications or skills I didn't have. So it would have to be another boring admin job. But after reading a dozen ads for those, it became clear I wasn't qualified to apply for the same job I'd been doing for the last ten years. Even the entry-level positions required university degrees or internet technology certificates, or any of a dozen other things I didn't have.

I slammed down the laptop lid, too panicked to think. Breathe, I told myself. It wasn't as bad as it seemed. It was just an off day. Tomorrow, there would be positions I could apply for. My heart raced, I was almost hyperventilating, and I had the weirdest feeling that I wasn't alone. But the doors were locked — I never left them unlocked, ever — and however shabby the house was, it did at least have security screens on all the windows. So it wasn't possible for there to be someone else in the house. But still the feeling persisted and I found myself turning to look over my shoulder a couple of times, certain that somebody stood right behind me.

Once I had myself back under control, I opened the laptop again and picked out a couple of jobs to apply for. I had to fudge my experience a little, but hopefully I'd get at least one interview. If I could get through to an interview, I was pretty sure I could convince them to hire me.

Feeling more optimistic, I went upstairs to check my wardrobe. It wouldn't hurt to put together one or two interview outfits now. That way, when the calls started coming, I'd be ready. I had a couple of nice suits I hadn't worn for years: a navy pantsuit, and a black skirt and jacket, which I usually wore with a white tailored shirt. But when I pulled them out of the wardrobe, it was clear they weren't going to fit. Nevertheless, I valiantly tried to squeeze myself into them. I couldn't get the navy pants up over my hips. I could get the skirt on, but there was zero chance of zipping it up, and both jackets strained at the seams.

"Oh, come on."

I threw the clothes onto my bed and rubbed my watery eyes. Allergies. I definitely wasn't crying. Okay, so it would probably be at least a week before any interviews. There was time to lose some weight. Maybe not as much as it would take to fit into my old interview clothes, but if I could squeeze into one of the jackets, I could wear it with a pair of my black work trousers.

No time like the present to get started, so I grabbed my sneakers and headed out for a brisk walk. It was pretty hot outside and I was nowhere near as fit as I used to be, so my brisk walk turned into a slow trudge around the block. By the time I got home, I was red faced, dripping sweat, and panting. At least it was a start.

By the time Saturday rolled around, I felt pretty good. I had spent each morning applying for positions. I ate salads for lunch and spent the afternoons reading motivational books I downloaded from online. You know the kind — you can change your life rah rah rah. I normally can't stand them, but if I was ever going to make a big change, this was the time to do it. When the afternoon heat started to ease, I went for a thirty-minute walk. It still wasn't a brisk walk, but it was getting a little easier. It had been years since I thought about my diet or my health and this brief interlude while I was between jobs was the perfect time to form some better habits.

The voices hadn't spoken again, for which I was immensely thankful. They probably indicated some sort of mental break-down, but hopefully I had averted it. I just needed to stay positive, eat right, and exercise. Surely it wasn't possible to have a mental breakdown while doing all those things.

So that Saturday morning, I ate my poached eggs on sour-dough and thought life was getting back on track — until I checked my emails and realised I had six rejections for the positions I had applied for. Six and not a single interview. That was when I realised just how much trouble I was in. I was thirty-five, unemployed, and had a mortgage. The redundancy package Mac had promised turned out to be ten weeks' pay. One week for each year I worked for him. It was hardly generous and I wondered whether it even met any legal requirements, but there was no point trying to find out. I didn't have the energy to fight him.

What was I going to do? Sure, a couple of those rejections were for jobs I hadn't thought I had much chance at, but four were ones I could do in my sleep. Maybe no employer wanted somebody my age, despite my experience. They wanted the fresh young graduates. The ones with fancy degrees and the kind of IT experience I couldn't even imagine. I didn't know how to create Facebook ads and I didn't have a clue what a PPC ad was. I had never maintained a website, written a blog, or uploaded a YouTube video, and I didn't even know what a VA was, let alone have any experience. How on earth would I ever find another job?

For a few horrible minutes, I thought about ringing Mac and begging him to give me back my job. I could blackmail him about his affair. My mobile phone was in my hand before I came to my senses. No, I wouldn't call Mac. I wouldn't beg. Yes, I was in a mess, but I would find my own way out of it. And I would start by cleaning the house.

I hauled the vacuum cleaner out of the hall cupboard and ran it over the threadbare carpet in the lounge room. I had initially thought I might use my redundancy package for some new carpet. I had dreamed about replacing the old couch and wondered whether I might even have enough money left over to get in a painter. Now it seemed the best I could do was clean the walls.

Like my health, house maintenance was something else I had paid little attention to. I had lived in this house for almost as long as I had worked for Mac and it needed painting when I bought it. I'd never had any spare money for that sort of thing, though. My lack of cash also meant I didn't have much furniture, so vacuuming was easy. Just the old couch, its black leather now splitting at the seams and one side sagging, a small cabinet on which sat a TV — an old, boxy one, not one of those modern flat screens — and a stained glass lamp I picked up cheap at a market.

Absorbed in my thoughts, it wasn't until I switched off the vacuum cleaner that I noticed the voices arguing. I had been hearing them for a while, just faintly over the sound of the vacuum, but had taken no notice. I listened for a while but couldn't make any sense of their argument. There were three voices, maybe four if one didn't say much. I felt the creeping edge of a headache and wished they would go away. I couldn't afford a psychologist right now.

I wheeled the vacuum cleaner to my bedroom and got to work on the carpet in there. By the time I turned the vacuum off again, my head throbbed and the voices were still going. So much for heading off that breakdown. The voices kept arguing and my headache kept getting worse and worse. I finally snapped.

"For god's sake, will you shut up?"

The argument continued for a few seconds before it trailed off, the way a conversation dies when the person everyone's been bitching about walks into the room.

"Did you hear that?" one of them asked.

There was a long pause, then several voices at once.

"Did she—"

"I told—"

"What the—"

"Enough!" A woman's voice. Confident, bossy. The others hushed. "Just give her a minute."

Goosebumps pimpled my arms and legs, and I would have sworn I could feel eyes boring into me. I even checked behind me, making sure I really was alone.

"Maybe she got us for a moment," a male voice said after a while. "Happened before with others. Never lasts long."

I left the vacuum cleaner and went to find the ibuprofen I had bought years ago during a bout of the flu. It was probably expired by now, but it would be better than nothing.

"I think we've lost her," someone said.

I didn't bother to reply. Engaging in a conversation with the voices wouldn't do anything good for my mental state. First thing Monday morning, I'd make a psychologist appointment. Or a psychiatrist. I wasn't sure which was which.

But when Monday rolled around, I discovered it wasn't that easy to get an appointment with either a psychologist or a psychiatrist. Turned out I needed a referral from a doctor first, or at least I did if I wanted a Medicare-subsidised appointment. I found an online directory of doctor's clinics and made an appointment at the nearest one.

It was only as I waited in the clinic's reception that I wondered what to say to the doctor. I didn't want to tell a stranger that I had been hearing voices. Perhaps I could just say I had lost my job and was feeling very stressed. Surely that would be enough to get a referral.

But the doctor didn't agree. She offered me a prescription for antidepressants and recommended I eat better, cut down on caffeine, and get more exercise. She also suggested I get away for a few days, despite my having already told her I worried about not being able to pay my mortgage.

When I asked for a referral to a psychologist, she told me to try the things she had suggested first and come back in a month if I still wanted the referral. I finally told her I had been hearing voices, but she didn't seem to believe me. Maybe she thought I was making it up to get the referral.

Eventually, I took the prescription she offered and left. I tossed it in the bin as soon as I got home. I was pretty sure that antidepressants would not make the voices go away.

CHAPTER
FOUR

A week passed before I heard the voices again. I had been sitting on the couch, flicking through the television channels, and I turned off the television just as they started.

"I wish she could still hear us." The girl, her voice wistful.

"You know it's not supposed to happen." The bossy woman. "She probably won't ever hear us again."

A sigh. "I know, but it was nice to think that somebody knew we were here. Even if it was just for a moment."

"No point wanting what we can't have." The older male, the one who didn't speak much.

"You've got us, Lis." The other male.

"I can still hear you," I said.

I don't know why I spoke to them. At that point, I still thought I was having a breakdown.

Silence.

Then pandemonium erupted.

"Oh my good—"

"I don't believe—"

"I told you she heard me the other day."

"Everyone be quiet." The bossy woman again. "This is going to be difficult enough without you all getting over excited. She's going to get a shock when she realises."

"When I realise what?" I rubbed my forehead. I needed ibuprofen. And wine. Maybe together. Perhaps I shouldn't have thrown out that prescription.

There was something that sounded like hurried whispers, before bossy woman spoke again.

"Dorothy, my name's Bec."

I didn't even have time to wonder how bossy woman knew my name before the other voices chimed in.

"Hi Dorothy, I'm Lissa."

"I'm Gray."

A pause. "I'm Samson."

"Where are you? And can you please go back to wherever you usually are? You know, wherever it is that I can't hear you. I know it's not normal to hear invisible people, but the doctor didn't believe me, so I would just like you all to go away."

It was Bec who answered. She was obviously the one in charge. I already had a mental image of her. Forty-something, hair that didn't dare disobey, a lived-in face.

"Dorothy, where do you think we might be?"

My head pounded in time with my pulse. I went to the kitchen to find the ibuprofen. I must remember to buy more.

"I'm not really in the mood for games," I said. "If you want to tell me where you are, go ahead. Otherwise, can you please be quiet?"

"Would it surprise you if I said we were in the kitchen with you?" Bec asked.

Although I knew she was lying, I did look around the room. It was starting to sparkle around the edges. That headache was turning into a migraine.

"Then why can't I see you?" I popped the ibuprofen out of

its blister pack and washed it down with tap water. I eyed the wine rack, but it wasn't even noon.

"It's kind of a long story." One of the male voices. Gray, I thought. I could picture him too: early thirties, strong jaw. The one who had told me about Mac's baby. "Maybe you should sit down."

"Maybe you should just leave me in peace." I'll be damned if I was going to be bossed around by some breakdown-induced invisible person.

The voices whispered between themselves. Assuming they had selves, that is.

"It's rude to talk about people when they're in the room." I went to my bedroom, drew the curtains closed, and climbed into bed.

The air rustled and I had a brief, vivid image of four people surrounding me. Two perched on the bed with me, one on either side. One sat on the carpet, cross-legged like a schoolgirl, and one stood, legs wide, hands clasped behind his back. I blinked and the image disappeared before I had even seen it properly. I would make an appointment with a different doctor first thing tomorrow. Whatever brand of psychosis I was experiencing, it was progressing fast if I had gone from hearing voices to seeing people who appeared and disappeared.

"Dorothy, we are going to tell you something you might find disturbing," Bec said. For just a moment, I thought I saw her again, sitting beside me on the bed. "You might find this hard to believe."

"Maybe later." I put a pillow over my head to block out the light — and the imaginary people.

"We are spirits," she said. "For some reason, we haven't crossed over. In fact, we aren't even sure we're supposed to cross over. We seem to be stuck here."

I knocked off the pillow and sat up so quickly that the room spun around me. The sparkles got brighter and my head pounded even harder. Was it possible for a migraine to trigger a brain haemorrhage?

"What do you mean, you're stuck here? In my house?"

If I hadn't been so preoccupied with the pain in my head, the shrillness of my voice might have embarrassed me.

"Sort of," Bec said. "If we leave the house, we can only go a few paces towards the road and then we get brought back."

"Except for Gray." Lissa. Teenage, curly blonde ringlets, a chubby cherub face. "He can go wherever you do."

I couldn't think through the pulsing pain. The room was fuzzy around the edges, but I could still see enough to know that I was indeed alone.

"You okay, Dorothy?" The fourth voice. Samson. A big black man with small, delicate hands. It was strange that I could see his hands so clearly when the rest of him was blurry.

"Spirits." I tried not to choke on the word. "Do you mean you're ghosts?"

"We prefer spirits." Bec again. "Ghosts sounds so airy fairy."

I lay back down, carefully so I didn't jar my head. Maybe it was a stroke. Were headaches a sign of stroke?

"Or souls." Lissa's voice was hesitant. "I wouldn't mind souls."

"Spirits." Bec's tone left no room for argument.

"Of course, spirits is best," Lissa said.

"Does that mean you're..." What if they didn't know?

"Are we dead?" Gray asked. "Yes, I'm afraid we are."

"How long?"

I could almost see him shrug. He was fuzzier than the others and I didn't quite get a good look at him, only his silhouette. It was funny the way I saw those brief, flickering images of them, like a TV on the blink. I never saw them like that again. Perhaps the connection was stronger that day. Or maybe I was meant to see them, just a glimpse so I could picture the spirits that would become such a big part of my life.

"We don't know," Gray said. "Time is different on this side of the veil."

"The veil?"

"It's what separates us from you," Lissa said. "It's like a big curtain of clouds hanging down from the sky."

"It doesn't look solid," Gray said. "But it's rock hard to touch."

"And you can see me through it?"

"Only when you're in the house," Bec said. "When you leave, the veil gets thicker."

"Except for Gray," Lissa said. "He can see you anywhere. That's why we think he's tied to you, rather than the house."

"Is Gray the voice that spoke to me at work?"

Why was I still talking to them? Surely this was something you weren't supposed to do when you had a breakdown, but I didn't seem to be able to stop. I was probably encouraging my psychosis, or something. It wasn't like my house was actually full of ghosts. Spirits. My stomach cramped and I made it to the bathroom just in time to toss my poached eggs into the toilet.

When I stopped heaving, I rinsed my face at the sink. It was the pain that made me sick. Everyone knows that pain causes nausea. I stumbled back to my bed and put the pillow over my head again.

"You can go away now," I said.

CHAPTER

FIVE

When I woke the next morning, both my headache and the invisible people were gone. I breathed a sigh of relief. Maybe I wasn't insane yet. I made a cup of tea and a mental note to buy coffee, then opened my laptop.

I had always intended to set up a proper home office, something cosy and inviting where I could deal with Mac's last-minute tasks from home instead of staying late at work. The spare bedroom would have been a suitable spot, but I had never got around to it. Instead, my "office" comprised one end of the kitchen counter, a bar stool, my old laptop and a small printer.

I scrolled through all the usual job vacancy sites, feeling increasingly despondent. More of the same jobs I could do in my sleep but apparently wasn't qualified for. Three more rejections waited in my inbox by the time I felt brave enough to check. My vision blurred as I read them. The monthly mortgage payment was due tomorrow. I had enough money for that one, and the next, but then I'd be in trouble. I had worked since I was eighteen. There had to be something I was qualified for.

I had an uneasy feeling that someone was in the room with

me. It wasn't possible, and I refused to let myself look over my shoulder. But the hairs on my arms stood up and the longer I spent not looking behind me, the more uneasy I grew. When someone cleared their throat, I jumped and almost fell off the bar stool.

"Calm down, Dorothy," I said to myself. "You're having a mental breakdown. Imaginary people, mysterious voices. You're lonely and miserable. That's all."

"I guess we are invisible to you," a female voice said. "But we aren't really."

A chill ran through me. That she sounded too young to be dangerous didn't make any difference. There really was an invisible person in my kitchen.

"Don't come any closer." I scrabbled across the counter, searching for a weapon. A knife would be nice, or a frying pan. My fingers landed on something. "I have a... pen."

"I've been dead for a while, but even in my time, we didn't consider a pen dangerous." My original invisible friend, sounding almost amused.

I say almost because it was difficult to tell whether the smirk in his voice was amusement or mocking. He was the one my psychosis had named Gray. The girl was Lissa.

"How do you know I don't have a knife in my other hand?"

I edged towards the kitchen drawers. The invisible people were close — my kitchen wasn't large, after all. Maybe six or seven paces away. Could I get to the knife drawer and find a weapon before they attacked me?

"We're invisible," Gray said. "Not blind."

No point trying to do it surreptitiously in that case. I rushed over, dragged open the drawer, and grabbed the first thing my hand landed on. It turned out to be a satisfactorily large carving knife. I held it up in front of me and the blade quivered as I pointed it around the empty kitchen.

"Stay where you are. I'm calling the police."

"To tell them what, exactly?" Bossy woman. Bec. "That you have a kitchen full of invisible people? Do you think the police will take you seriously? Especially when you tell them you're recently unemployed and in a dubious mental state?"

"Harsh, Bec," Lissa said. "She's having a rough time."

"Have you been spying on me?" Now I didn't know whether to be afraid or angry. "How many of you are there, and why are you here?"

"We've already told you who we are." Bec again. "Don't you remember?"

"That was a hallucination."

I wasn't feeling so certain anymore, though. It had happened too many times. I was completely sober and speaking to three invisible people.

"So what do you call a hallucination when it continues?" Gray asked. "Surely you must have started thinking we might be real."

I shrugged and clutched the knife a little harder. I would stab them if they came any closer, although my hands shook so much that I was just as likely to drop the knife. I could only hope invisible people had bodies that could be stabbed.

"You don't have to get huffy," Bec said with a sniff. "We know when we're not wanted."

They didn't speak again. I waited for a while, and the knife grew sweaty in my hand, but they didn't make another peep.

"Hello?" I said. "Are you still here?"

They didn't reply and, strangely, I found myself almost disappointed.

CHAPTER
SIX

A week went by, then another. The rejections continued to appear in my inbox, but I also submitted an awful lot of applications with no response. One day when I felt brave, I rang two of the companies to enquire. One told me snottily that if I hadn't received a response, then I hadn't been shortlisted. The other said they would contact me if there was any information available. I didn't have the courage to ring anyone else after that.

To distract myself, I kept busy with trying to lose weight and stave off my mental breakdown. I ate salads, somewhat shocked at just how expensive it was to eat healthy. I went for walks and did step ups on my front stairs and sit ups in my living room. The scales showed a slightly lower weight, and that buoyed me enough to continue my efforts.

I was lonely, though, and bored out of my brain. I couldn't stand to watch any more daytime television, although I did catch a few episodes of *The Sophia Show*. The host, Sophia, was a household name. Even I had heard of her although I had never seen her show before. The audience went crazy every time she appeared on stage and I couldn't quite figure out why, even after sitting through four episodes. It was just another gossipy celebrity interview show. There seemed to be one of them on every channel at some point through the afternoon.

I went to the library, but I didn't really know what sort of books I might like and everything I tried was either too dull to keep my attention or too intricate to follow. The invisible people hadn't spoken again so it seemed I had avoided a total mental breakdown. Or so I thought.

It was a stinking hot day, even for February in Brisbane, Australia. By mid-afternoon, I was going stir-crazy rattling around the house, so I braved the heat to go for a walk. I underestimated the humidity, though. I was only halfway around the circuit I usually took when my water bottle ran dry. The sun was relentless and it was that time of the afternoon when there is no shade and not even the slightest gasp of a breeze.

My head pounded and my stomach churned. I wasn't sweating anymore, which I was pretty sure wasn't a good sign. I finally came across a tree that provided the tiniest patch of shade, barely large enough to huddle into. I leaned against its rough trunk and hoped I wasn't about to vomit on someone's front lawn.

The longer I stood there, the worse I felt. The only way I would get home was to keep walking, so I left the meagre shade and continued on. My legs wobbled and the world tilted from side to side. The grass crunched under my sneakers when I wandered off the footpath and a lone magpie watched me from its perch on a fence, its beak wide open as it gasped for breath.

I had to stop twice more, although I couldn't find any shade. I leaned against someone's front fence for a while, and against a sturdy brick mailbox another time. My heart seemed to beat way too hard. Heat stroke, heat exhaustion. I could never remember which was which, but I definitely had one of them.

By the time I got home, my vision was swimming and I

could barely focus my eyes long enough to get the key into the lock. I burst through the front door and leaned against the wall. Shade, blessed shade. It had to be at least ten degrees cooler in here.

I drank a glass of water straight from the kitchen tap, although it was almost too hot to swallow. With my glass refilled, and this time with a few ice cubes, I made my way unsteadily to my bedroom, which was the only room with air conditioning. I turned on the air and pulled off my sweaty clothes. I almost couldn't be bothered having a shower but it would cool me down quickly, so I wobbled into the bathroom. The water from the cold tap was as hot as it had been in the kitchen.

As the water sluiced over me, my head cleared. I gulped down mouthfuls of water until my stomach cramped and I realised I had probably had too much too soon. I longed to sit down in the shower and let the water continue to pour over me, but I wasn't sure I would get up again if I did.

The bedroom had cooled somewhat by the time I returned and I toppled onto my bed. The room pulsed in time with my heartbeat and little sparkles appeared around the edges of my vision. My head throbbed, also in time with my heart, but it didn't hurt as badly if I didn't move.

"Is she all right?" a voice asked. It was the invisible person my psychosis had named Lissa.

"She overdid it. It looks hot out there today." Bec, if I recalled correctly. "Silly woman. She should know better at her age."

"She's trying so hard to lose weight," Lissa said. "Poor thing."

"She's done all the right things now, though." The younger male, Gray. "She'll cool down quick enough. As long as she keeps up the fluids, she should be okay."

Fluids. Water. I should have some more. I cracked one eye open just enough to find the glass and drank a few sips.

"Shouldn't have been out in the heat today if it's as hot as it looks," Bec said.

"Give it a rest, Bec," Gray said.

"She should be more sensible. She knows better than that."

The two of them bickered for a while, with an occasional interjection from Lissa. I tried to tune them out and go to sleep, but their voices grew louder and louder. My headache was getting worse and all I could think about was stopping the noise. I didn't even care if it meant I was having a breakdown. I just wanted them to stop.

"Would you shut up?" I snapped.

The argument died in mid-sentence.

"She heard us again." Lissa, her voice wondering.

"What has changed? Why does she hear us sometimes, but not others?" Gray asked.

"She's probably responding to vibrations or something," Bec said. "I doubt she's actually hearing us again. You know it doesn't happen that often."

"Yes, I can hear you," I said. "It would be hard to miss the constant arguing. Now would you please shut up and go back to wherever it is that I can't hear you?"

Silence. Beautiful silence. For all of about a minute.

"Dorothy—" Bec started.

"For the love of god." I sat up and glared around the room. It tilted from side to side and stars sparkled around the edges. "How many times do I have to say it? Just. Shut. Up."

Silence. I waited, still glaring around the room, but the invisible people didn't speak again and eventually I flopped back down and closed my eyes.

I didn't let myself think about whether it was normal for imaginary people to do what they were told.

CHAPTER

SEVEN

I slept for the rest of the afternoon and through most of the night, but by four a.m. I was wide awake. The nausea had settled and my headache was little more than a dull throb. As I got out of bed, I still felt fragile, but I was pretty sure I was going to live.

In the kitchen, I flipped open my laptop while I waited for my tea. The notification on my inbox showed five unread messages. I couldn't look at them yet. Instead, I went to one of the job sites and scrolled through the new ads. By the time my tea was ready, I had confirmed there was absolutely nothing I could apply for. I took a deep breath to steady myself and opened my inbox. Form rejections. Every one of them. My eyes burned and I quickly closed my emails. I took a deep breath. What was I going to do?

I scrolled through the vacancies, desperately hoping for something new. Something I was actually qualified for. My gaze fell on an ad off to the side. One of those weird ones that has nothing to do with the page you're looking at. They're usually for bikinis or kitchen appliances or something equally useless. The heading on this one was *Genuine Clairvoyant.*

Do you have unfinished business with someone who has passed? I can help you speak with them. Call Mona now!

Beneath that was a Brisbane phone number and Mona's fee: one hundred dollars. How many suckers did she draw in each week? An ad like this probably wasn't cheap. I turned my attention back to the vacancies and when I scrolled down, Mona's ad disappeared.

I applied for three more positions, although I didn't feel hopeful about any of them. How was it possible that the world had moved on so much in just ten years? The last time I applied for a job — when Mac hired me — there had been plenty of suitable positions. In fact, I had agonised over whether to accept Mac's offer or hold out for another I had interviewed for. The other company spent too long in making a decision and by the time they offered me the job, I had given up waiting and accepted Mac's. And I mostly hadn't regretted it until the day he fired me.

Mona's ad seemed permanently fixed to every job site I looked at after that. I continued to hear the invisible people over the next few days, although I pretended I didn't. I considered ringing Mona to ask if she too heard invisible people who claimed to be ghosts, but figured she probably got all sorts of crackpot phone calls.

As I tabbed from website to website, searching for anything I might possibly apply for, I caught sight of another ad. *Do you hear voices?* the headline screamed. *Why yes, I do,* I muttered as I clicked on the ad.

Seeing things that shouldn't be there? Are you experiencing things that other people call hallucinations, delusions, or paranoia? Our amber beads can help.
Our patented amber beads will block your connection with the spirits

that are trying to ruin your life. For only $49.95, what do you have to lose?

Just my money, I figured. My sanity was already gone. I lingered over the ad, sorely tempted. It was only when I zoomed in to take a closer look that I saw the fine print at the bottom: *Not intended as a treatment for clinically diagnosed schizophrenia.*

My heart skipped a beat. Schizophrenia. Why hadn't I thought of that? All this time I thought I was having some kind of breakdown, but maybe it was schizophrenia. I opened a new browser tab and searched for symptoms of schizophrenia. Hallucinations, delusions, inability to concentrate, memory problems, emotional withdrawal. Yep, I had all of those.

Another search revealed that schizophrenia was usually diagnosed in the mid to late twenties, but some people might not be diagnosed until their mid-thirties. That was me. Thirty-five.

Treatment for schizophrenia: antipsychotic medications and psychotherapy.

Is there a cure for schizophrenia? No.

I lingered on that page, not wanting to believe what I read. Could my life get any worse? I was unemployed and fast approaching broke. I only had enough money to last another few weeks. If I didn't find a job before then, I didn't know what I would do. My house might not be much, but at least I wasn't homeless. And now I was schizophrenic.

Take a deep breath, Dorothy. Something would come up sooner or later. I wasn't going to lose the house. In the meantime, I had to make the last of my payout stretch further. So forget the salads. They were too expensive. I would eat as cheaply as I could. But even so, I couldn't eat little enough to cover an extra mortgage payment. I needed a job, and fast.

Three more rejections arrived in my inbox on Tuesday morning. I tried not to fall apart as I read them. I had applied for dozens of jobs and had received nothing other than form rejections. Not a single interview. Not even a phone call.

There was nothing I could apply for today. Not even if I fudged my experience. Every position needed some kind of qualification I didn't have. If I couldn't find a job working for someone else, maybe I could create a job. Run my own business. For a few moments, I lost myself in a fantasy of being my own boss. Setting my own hours and controlling my time. Being a businesswoman. A small business owner. Maybe I could offer some kind of remote secretarial services. There must be people who wanted things typed but didn't need someone to come into an office all day.

Inspired, I searched online for dictation services. I found a company that offered typists to transcribe audio files. Surely I was perfectly qualified for that after all those letters I had typed for Mac. I clicked on the "work for us" tab — and was quickly disillusioned.

For starters, I couldn't type fast enough. They wanted a minimum typing speed of a hundred words a minute. I was an adequate typist, but I could only do about seventy words a minute. Also, the pay was so lousy that I wouldn't be able to cover my mortgage, even if I worked sixty hours a week. The customer paid a cent per word and the typist received a fraction of that.

But back to my small business owner idea. Maybe rather than working for somebody else, I could offer my own typing services. If I charged a cent a word and got to keep it all, I could make enough. I would have to maintain my usual seventy words a minute all day, and I'd have to secure enough clients to keep me busy, but even if I only had a couple to start with, at least it would mean some money coming in. That would be a far better situation than what I was in right now.

My gaze landed on Mona's ad, which somehow seemed to be on practically every website I looked at. I scoffed as I read it again. At least typing was honest work. Mona made her money by lying to people. All clairvoyants were fakes. Everyone who consulted with them knew that, even if they pretended to believe. It must be easy money, though. All you had to do was tell a bit of a story, let people think you'd passed on a message for them, then take their hundred dollars. Maybe I could try that if the typing didn't work out.

What was I thinking? Mona defrauded people. Pretended to be something she wasn't. Pretended she had some connection with their deceased loved ones. I couldn't do it. Not even to keep my house. I would sleep on the streets before I set out to deceive anyone.

I spent the rest of the morning crafting an advertisement for my typing services. I agonised over the wording. Should I offer a guarantee on maximum turnaround time? An express service for urgent jobs? For a premium rate, of course. A guarantee of accuracy? After several hours, I finally had something I was happy with.

I found a website that allowed freelancers to advertise their services and created an account. That was when I received the next nasty shock: the fee to advertise with them was prohibitive. If I didn't eat for the next two weeks, I still wouldn't have enough money left to both make my next mortgage payment and pay for an ad for even five days. I checked a couple of other similar sites and they were all just as expensive. How would I find any clients if I couldn't afford to advertise my services?

A quick internet search for "cheap ways to advertise" elicited a suggestion to put up notices at local shops. That was something I could do. I prettied up my ad as best I could with a border and some clip art, then printed half a dozen copies. Once it was cool enough to venture outside, I walked my print-outs down to the local supermarket and plastered the community noticeboard. I crossed my fingers and hoped some work would come in soon.

EIGHT

It was Saturday morning before the first phone call about my ad.

"Your prices are pretty expensive," he said.

"They're industry standard." I tried to keep my voice even and confident. That was what people wanted when they hired a freelancer. Calm, unflappable.

"Tell you what," he said. "I'll make you a deal. I'll pay a third of a cent per word and I'll throw in some free promotion. That's a pretty good deal for you. I wouldn't normally make an offer like this."

"I really can't discount my prices," I said. "I have a mortgage to pay."

"Well, sorry, but I can't pay what you're asking. A third of a cent is my best offer."

"Thank you for your call, then."

I hung up before he could say anything else. I fumed for a while, then figured I may as well check the job ads. Once again, there was nothing I could apply for. My gaze landed on Mona's ad. I clicked on it, although I had read it so many times I even knew her phone number by heart.

"You look at that ad a lot," the voice that called itself Gray said.

He sounded close, like he stood right behind me. I resisted the urge to look over my shoulder.

"I think I know why," he continued.

"Of course you do. You're inside my head."

A snort of laughter.

"You still think you're having some sort of breakdown? You're too sensible for that, Dorothy. I think you know the truth and that's why you keep looking at that ad. I'm only surprised you haven't admitted it yet."

"Admitted what?"

I may as well listen. My delusion might have some useful advice for me. Something my subconscious self had figured out, but my conscious self was still ignoring. Maybe that's why the voices kept returning. I had to let them say what they were here for before they would go away.

"Realised the truth about what we are. Where we are. We tried to tell you, but you didn't listen."

"I already know what you are," I said. "And I don't like what that says about my mental health, so I'm pretending it's not happening."

"How can I prove that we're as real as you are?"

"I don't know. Tell me something that nobody but me would know. Wait, that won't work. If you're inside my head, you already know everything I know. How about you make something move?"

"I wish I could." He sounded genuinely regretful. "But we can't impact on the physical world. Believe me, we've tried."

"Then I guess I'll just have to keep on thinking that you're a delusion."

"Have you ever lost someone, Dorothy?"

I jumped off the bar stool and slammed the laptop shut.

"That's low," I snapped. "Considering you're in my head, you already know the answer to that."

"Who is it? What if I could find that person and relay a message from them? Would you believe me then?"

I was tempted. Sorely tempted.

"No," I said. "Don't ask me that."

"Then what can I say to make you believe me?"

Bec interrupted before I could reply. I hadn't even realised she was there. In as much as an invisible person can be somewhere.

"I don't know why you're bothering," she said with a huff.

"I'm bothering because we can help her," he said. "Why shouldn't I offer?"

"She lost her brother," Bec said. "I think it happened before you arrived. I can't be sure of the timing, of course, but it makes sense of why you didn't know. But anyway, we should have discussed it before you offered."

"You don't have to be involved," he said. "I'll do it."

"Do what?" I asked, partly out of curiosity and partly to head off the argument.

Lord, how far gone was I to be intervening in bickering between my imaginary friends?

"I can contact your brother for you, Dorothy," Gray said.

"Go away," I said. "If you're inside my head, you know how much that still hurts."

"*If* I'm inside your head? That's the first time you've admitted that maybe I'm not."

"Go. Away."

He didn't speak again, but I was too wound up to focus on job ads now. Surely the fact that I was having entire conversations with invisible friends suggested schizophrenia rather than a breakdown. I'd have to go back to the doctor.

Since the previous doctor didn't believe me, I made an

appointment with a different clinic. This time I started with a brief explanation of how I had lost my job, was very stressed, and had started hearing voices.

"What kind of things do the voices say?" the doctor asked.

I hadn't expected that. Surely saying I had been hearing voices should be enough.

"They're trying to convince me they're real," I said. "That they aren't just inside my head, but they live in my house."

"And do you ever see any of the people these voices belong to?" she asked.

"No." That one time surely didn't count.

"And who do you think the voices belong to?"

"I don't know. They've all given me their names, but I don't think I know any of them, if that's what you mean."

She gave me an odd look, as if I had said the wrong thing.

"How many voices are there?" she asked.

"Four?" Maybe I should have said one. Or two. Four might be pretty bad.

Her eyes narrowed. "You don't sound like you're sure about that."

"There's four."

She asked a few more questions, then handed me a prescription and a referral for a psychiatrist. I went straight to the pharmacy next door. While I waited for them to fill the prescription, I wandered around the shop. Blood pressure monitors, vitamins, shampoos, lip balms. Nothing I needed, and I had to be careful about what I spent until I could find some work again. The psychiatrist appointment wasn't going to be cheap.

"I can't believe you still don't think we're real," Gray said.

I shot a glance over my shoulder, even though I already knew there wasn't anyone there.

"I've offered to contact your brother for you. What else can I do to convince you?"

"You aren't real," I whispered. "Once I take this new medication, you'll disappear."

"Why are you talking to me if I'm not real?" he asked. "If you're so sure I'm in your head, why don't you just think your reply?"

Fine, go away.

He didn't respond.

I wandered a little further down the aisle.

"How's the job hunting going?" Gray asked.

"I thought I told you to go away."

"If you did, I didn't hear you. Any chance you thought it instead of saying it? Since I'm not in your head, I don't know what you're thinking."

I inhaled and tried to exhale my annoyance away. I should have asked the doctor whether stress could induce schizophrenia or if it was genetic.

"Why didn't you tell the doctor that we're spirits?" Gray asked. "Not criticising you or anything, but it seems like important information."

"How do you know what I told the doctor?" I asked.

"I was there. I didn't want to distract you, though."

"You were listening in on my doctor's appointment? That was private."

"If it was so private, you could have told me not to go. I would have respected that if you did. But since you were there to talk about us, I think we have a right to know what you're saying."

"You don't have any rights. You don't even exist."

"I know you're only saying that because you're trying to convince yourself, but it's really hurtful. Think how you would feel if you were dead and someone kept saying you don't exist. I can see I'm wasting my time here. I'm going back to the house."

I felt a pang of guilt, which I chided myself for. I had enough problems without feeling bad about hurting imaginary people. But he had sounded so wounded. Was there any possibility — any at all — that the voices were real?

"Dorothy Marks!" The pharmacist sounded irritated, as if she had been calling me for a while.

What if it wasn't just in my head? If the voices were real, taking the medication wouldn't help and I couldn't afford to buy something I didn't need.

The pharmacist called my name again, but I ducked my head down and hurried out. I would think about it overnight. I could always come back tomorrow and pick up the medication.

CHAPTER
NINE

I checked the vacancies again when I got home. I had given up on the idea of an admin job. Now I was applying for supermarkets and restaurants. Even a position as an office night cleaner. I couldn't afford to be fussy. I jumped at Lissa's voice.

"Gray is pretty upset with you, Dorothy," she said.

"Don't do that," I snapped.

"Do what?"

"Sneak up on me like that."

A long pause.

"I can't help it. You don't seem to realise I'm here unless I speak."

"So how often are you here but don't say anything?"

Another pause.

"We're always here. Kind of. We live here."

I sighed. There was no point arguing with myself or my consciousness or whatever the voices were.

"So what happened with Gray?" she asked. "Did you guys have a fight?"

"Sort of."

"He's really upset."

"Yeah, you said that."

"Like, really upset. I think you should apologise to him."

"Fine, I'll apologise next time I see him. Hear him. Whatever."

I spotted Mona's ad again and clicked on it without thinking. It was becoming a habit to read her ad every time I saw it.

"He says you don't believe we exist." Lissa's voice was very quiet. "Is that true?"

I closed the laptop. Did other people who had breakdowns or schizophrenia or whatever this was have such demanding invisible friends?

"We could find someone for you," she said. "Not your brother. You got upset when Gray suggested that. But someone else. Then you'd have to believe us."

"Lissa!" It was Bec. How long had she been listening? "We need to talk about things like that first."

"But she'll believe us if we do it," Lissa said. "Besides, Gray already offered."

"Maybe we should." That was Samson. "Seems everyone's spending a lot of energy tryin' to convince Dorothy we exist. Be good if we could get past that."

"Fine," I said. "Find me Clark Gable. Bring him to talk to me and maybe I'll believe you."

There was a moment of silence, then hurried whispering between the voices. At last Bec spoke.

"We don't think it works like that, Dorothy. You can't call just anyone. It has to be someone you know."

"Why?" I asked.

"We don't know. That's just how it works. We aren't even sure whether you can call anyone at all you know, or if it has to be someone who was close to you. Someone connected to you. We just know that you can't call a stranger."

"I'm not calling a stranger. Everyone knows Clark Gable."

"When you ask for someone you know, they hear you," she said. "They just... I don't know how to explain it, but they just arrive. We've seen it happen with other people who have lived here. Nobody has ever been able to communicate with the spirit they called, though. They never even knew the spirit came. The spirit can hear the living, but the living can't hear the spirit. Or at least, nobody has before. You're the first one to hear us, other than the odd moment. So if you call someone you knew and they come here, we can pass on whatever the spirit wants to say to you."

"That sounds ridiculous. And very complicated."

"Ridiculous or not, that's how it works." Bec's voice was frosty.

So now two of my imaginary friends were mad at me. Surely my subconscious could have invented imaginary people who were a bit easier to get along with.

"Okay then, how about you find my brother?" I regretted the words as soon as they were out of my mouth.

"What's his name?" Bec asked.

Tears filled my eyes and I sniffled a little. Hopefully, she was behind me and couldn't see me crying.

"Forget about it," I muttered.

"Dorothy, what's his name? We can't go on like this. If this is what it takes to convince you, let's just do it."

"Gary," I said. "Gary Marks."

Hurried whispering. An argument, by the sound of it.

"So," I asked. "Is he here?"

The whispering stopped.

"Anyone?" I asked.

But there was no reply. The voices seemed to be gone.

I didn't hear a peep out of my imaginary friends until the next morning when Gray cleared his throat behind me.

"Oh, good," I said. "More imaginary people who can't prove they exist."

"We apologise, Dorothy." His voice was stiff. "We couldn't find your brother."

"That's not how it works according to Bec. She said I only had to call and he would appear."

"Well, he didn't come and we don't know why. Maybe it means he's crossed over."

"Bec gave me the impression that any spirit that gets called just turns up. Why would my brother be any different?"

"We don't know. Sorry."

Then he was gone.

I opened my laptop. May as well apply for some jobs since it seemed like the invisible people were going to leave me alone for a while. The first thing I saw was Mona's ad.

Do you have unfinished business with someone who has passed? I can help you speak with them. Call Mona now!

Was there any chance Mona was genuine? Could she connect me with my brother? I'd always felt guilty that I didn't ring him as soon as I heard his message. Maybe things would have been different if I had. He might still be alive. If only I could tell him how sorry I was.

"Why don't you call her, Dorothy?" Lissa asked.

I should stop assuming I was ever alone.

"Why would I do that? She's a fake."

"You don't know that. She might be like you. Able to hear us."

I looked at the ad a little longer.

"Gray could go with you," she said. "You could ask Mona to contact him for you and see what happens."

"That's actually a pretty good idea." It was Gray.

I felt rather awkward that we had been talking about him without realising he was there. Or maybe Lissa knew. I might be the only one who was in the dark.

"Why would you do that?" I asked. "Go with me to see a clairvoyant."

"Because we need you to see that we're real," he said. "And I can't think of anything else. We've tried to convince you, but you won't listen. So maybe going to see Mona will help. Especially if she turns out to be real. If she can tell you what I'm saying, you'll hear it from both me and her. If she says what you just heard me say, surely then you'll believe."

It made sense, in a twisted sort of way. At least Mona's fee was cheaper than a psychiatrist.

"All right then," I said. "I'll call Mona."

TEN

For a genuine clairvoyant, Mona's schedule was surprisingly free and she was able to see me the next day. It was a bit of a hike across town to get to her. I had to catch two buses and then still walk a good way. Gray chattered a bit on the bus but was mostly silent as we walked. Well, I walked. I wasn't sure how he moved.

When we arrived at the address Mona had given me, I checked the details in my phone calendar twice. Her apartment building was even shabbier than my house, with paint peeling from every surface, long-rotted balcony railings, and a straggly patch of grass that was at least six weeks overdue for a mow.

I found a door with Mona's apartment number and knocked on it. Flakes of paint peeled off at my touch. Three bells on a red cord hung from the doorknob and I belatedly wondered whether I was supposed to have rung them.

The door opened and Mona peered short-sightedly out at me. She was younger than I had expected from her voice, not much older than myself, and would be quite pretty if she put on a pair of glasses so she didn't squint so badly. She wore jeans with the knees cut out and a singlet top, which didn't at all fit my expectation of how a clairvoyant would dress. Mona flicked a few strands of long blond hair off her face and smiled.

"Dorothy? Come in. I've been expecting you."

Of course you have. I made an appointment.

"Thank you."

Mona's front room was empty, except for two thick rugs separated by a low coffee table, and a very large, very conspicuous painting of a naked woman who appeared to be in the throes of ecstasy. I averted my gaze from the naked woman. Gray snorted, but I wasn't sure whether it was supposed to convey disgust or surprise.

"Please, Dorothy, be seated."

Mona eased herself down onto one rug and motioned towards the other. Following her example, I sat and crossed my legs like a schoolgirl. Three seconds later, my knees were screaming and all I wanted to do was stretch my legs. I wasn't sure I would be able to get up again without help.

The coffee table was bare except for a fat purple candle at either end, which Mona lit with a cigarette lighter. It was only then that I noticed the faint smell of cigarettes. Once I was aware of it, the smell became pervasive and irritating. Mona tossed the lighter onto the coffee table and smiled at me.

"Dorothy, how can I help you?"

"I'd like to contact a friend."

"A friend who has passed, I presume?"

I hesitated, wondering if the question was as dumb as it sounded. Why would I visit a clairvoyant to contact a living friend?

"That's right." A calm, bland answer in order to preserve my cover.

"And what is the name of this friend?"

"Gray."

"Gray what?"

I didn't know, but since I was pretty sure Mona was a fraud, I figured it didn't matter.

"Simpson." It was the first thing that popped into my head, probably because of that old *The Simpsons* episode I watched last night. Gray huffed and I focused on keeping a straight face.

"Gray Simpson." Mona's voice echoed through the room. "Gray Simpson, are you with us?"

"Sure am," Gray said.

"Gray. Simpson." She closed her eyes and rocked back and forth. "We seek contact with Gray Simpson."

"I already told you I'm here," he said.

Mona didn't react. Another few seconds passed.

"Ahh, there you are." She opened her eyes long enough to squint at me. "Dorothy, Gray says to tell you hello and he is glad you have sought him."

"Oh." I wondered what response she expected. "I'm glad I sought him too."

"So tell me, Dorothy." She closed her eyes again and resumed her back and forth rocking. "Who was Gray to you? He is telling me something, but I'm wondering whether you will say the same."

"I used to buy pigs from her," Gray said. "Nice, fat roasting pigs."

No flicker of reaction from Mona.

"A friend," I said.

"I'm thinking he must have been much more than a friend if you have gone to so much effort to seek him out."

"No, just a friend."

"That's not what Gray is telling me." Her voice was light and almost teasing. "He says you always told everyone you were just friends, but there were times where friends became so much more."

Gray snorted and it was only with difficulty that I restrained my smile.

"Well, there may have been the odd occasion when things between us became... steamy," I said.

Gray coughed, but Mona smiled.

"I thought as much."

Her voice was confident now, almost jubilant. She must have been thinking that she had pegged me right and knew exactly what I was here for.

"You were secret lovers, weren't you." It was a statement rather than a question.

Gray sounded like he was choking. I hesitated, wanting to seem as if I tiptoed around the question.

"I don't really want to discuss that. I'd just like to speak with Gray if he is here."

"Of course you do, my dear," Mona said. "And your Gray is right here with us. He tells me he's been waiting for you. That he couldn't cross over until he had spoken to you one last time. He says there are things you both need to say."

She smiled and waited for my reply. I had to hand it to her. She was good. Even though I knew that everything she had said so far was false, she almost had me believing that my secret lover, Gray, was there, just on the other side of the veil, waiting to speak with me one last time.

"You had better say something, Dorothy," Gray said, his voice dry. "I'm just gagging for it."

"I don't know what to say," I said.

"Just tell him whatever is in your heart," Mona said.

"Yeah, Dorothy, tell me what's in your heart," Gray echoed.

I badly wanted to say something inappropriate but resisted.

"I don't know what happened." It wasn't a lie, but I didn't mean it in the way Mona would think. "I don't know what I mean — meant — to him."

Mona rocked back and forth, eyes rolling up into her head. It went on for so long that I wondered whether she was having a seizure, but eventually she stopped and squinted at me.

"Gray has many things he wants to say," she said. "His biggest regret is that he never told you what you meant to him. He says he started to a number of times but could never do it."

She paused and I realised I was supposed to confirm her story. I nodded. Gray snorted.

"He says he regrets the way he left things between you. He wants you to know that he always loved you. It's this unresolved issue between the two of you that's stopping him from crossing over."

Again she waited.

"I see."

Gray laughed. "Where is she getting this stuff from? It's certainly not from me."

"Are you sure?" I asked.

Mona nodded. "Absolutely. Perhaps now that he has got this off his chest, he'll be able to cross over."

"It's just..." I paused to find the right words. Words that would show her I wanted to believe, but also that I didn't entirely buy her story. "It doesn't sound much like the Gray I know. Knew."

She rocked back and forth, eyes rolling. This seemed to be a stalling technique, something she used when she needed time to think up a response.

"Gray says there was more to him than you knew," she said. "There was a softer side that he rarely showed, although you glimpsed it a few times."

"Are you sure it's Gray you're hearing?" I asked.

Again, she rocked and rolled her eyes.

"It's definitely a masculine presence. Very strong, but somehow also comforting. He says his name is Gray Simpson and he recognises you, calling you by name. He says nobody else knew him the way you did and also that nobody knew just what things were really like between the two of you."

"And he's here right now, talking to you?"

Gray got the hint.

"Mona, is it? How you doing, Mona? I'm Gray, the one you're supposed to be contacting. It's not me you're relaying messages from, though. I'm not sure exactly who you're talking to since I'm the only spirit in the room."

Mona jumped a little and seemed to glance over her shoulder.

"You know, I think she's getting something from me," he said. "I don't think she hears me, but she's getting a vibe or something. She looks pretty freaked out."

He was right. Mona had stopped rolling her eyes and rocking and instead darted glances around the room. When Gray stopped talking, she took a deep breath.

"I'm sorry, Dorothy. Gray seems to have left us. Perhaps he has crossed over now that he has been able to tell you what he needed to."

"I'm right here," Gray said.

"Just like that?" I asked. "Is it possible to cross over so quickly?"

"Who knows how the ghostly plane works?" Mona got to her feet and I figured this must be a signal that my time was up. "We know so little of what happens to the ghosts of our dearly departed."

I handed over her fee and hobbled to the door. My legs were really unhappy about sitting like that for so long. Mona didn't bother to walk me out but stood by the coffee table and counted my twenties.

"Thank you." I paused in the doorway and looked back at her. "That was very... educational."

I turned to leave but stopped as if I'd just thought of something.

"Oh, by the way..."

Mona raised her eyebrows and arranged her face into an accommodating expression. She probably expected me to make another appointment. She seemed much calmer now that Gray had stopped talking.

"They prefer spirits."

Mona's face was blank.

"They don't like to be called ghosts. They prefer spirits."

Her face blanched.

"Bye Mona," Gray said.

As I closed the door behind me, Mona was darting glances around the room again.

"I should have asked her to tell me something that only you and I would know," I said as I walked back to the bus. My legs were loosening up, but I still couldn't walk very fast.

"She couldn't hear me, so it wouldn't have made any difference," Gray said. "It's a shame she's a fake. You didn't get what you were looking for."

"I suppose I kind of did." I spoke slowly, testing my thoughts before I shared them. "She seemed to pick up on you at the end. I feel like that was enough to confirm that you're not just my imagination."

"So what are we if you aren't imagining us?"

He was testing me. He wanted to hear me say it.

"I think you might be what you said you were. Spirits. Somehow living in my house."

He was silent for a while.

"I wasn't sure you would ever admit it," he said.

"I can't believe I am. How long have you been there?"

"Impossible to say. Less time than Bec and Lissa, longer than Samson."

"Do you remember much about your life?"

"Not really. None of us have much more than our names. I think I might have been military. Lissa remembers she was fifteen. Samson knows he was married at some point. Bec thinks she might have had a child although she can't remember whether it was a boy or a girl. We assume we aren't supposed to remember much. I suppose it's a way of making sure we let go of our lives."

"But why my house? Did you all live there?"

"I suppose that's the logical assumption. None of us have any specific memory of the house, but we must have either lived there or it was significant to us."

"Do you..." I hesitated, but he seemed to know what I wanted to ask.

"No," he said. "None of us have any memory of how we died."

"That's a good thing."

"I suppose. I think I would like to know, though."

"I could do some internet searches. There must be records of who owned the house previously. I might even be able to find your families."

"No, absolutely not. We've talked about it and agreed as a group that we wouldn't allow you to look for any information about our lives."

"But you just said you wanted to know how you died. I might at least be able to confirm whether you all lived in the house. Maybe get your last names and your ages."

"None of that matters," he said. "We are tied to the house and that's just the way it is. Except for me. I'm tied to you."

"Don't you want to know why?" I asked. "If I knew your full name, I might know who you are. I might remember something about you."

"No, Dorothy. Our lives are off limits. They're over and they need to stay in the past."

CHAPTER

ELEVEN

"Gray says you believe us now."

Lissa was already waiting for me as I let myself into the house.

"I suppose I do," I said.

"And you don't think you're going crazy anymore?"

"I don't think we're supposed to say crazy. It's not politically correct."

"Huh?"

So she hadn't died recently. Surely every twenty-first century teenager knew about political correctness.

"Never mind," I said.

I went to the kitchen and opened my laptop. May as well see if there were any other positions I could apply for. As I scrolled, Mona's ad appeared again and I couldn't stop myself from clicking on it.

"We have a proposal for you, Dorothy." Bec had arrived.

"Who's we?" I asked absently, absorbed with reading Mona's ad for the millionth time. How many clients a week did she see? How much did she make from her scam clairvoyant business?

"The four of us," Gray said.

"Are you all here?" I asked.

"Me and Samson are," Lissa said.

"Okay." I shut the laptop. "What's your proposal?"

"Gray told us about your visit with Mona," Bec said. "And that she couldn't hear him. So that got us thinking about a way we can help you. We know you're just about out of money and if you don't find a job soon, you might lose the house."

"How do you know all that?" I asked.

"You talk to yourself a lot," Lissa said. "Especially when you're looking at things on your computer."

"Anyway," Bec said. "As you are our only connection with the world of the living, we don't want that to happen. Also, if the house gets sold, we're concerned it might get knocked down. It's not in great condition, after all. And what would happen to us then? So we propose to help you make some money so you can keep the house."

"I'm listening," I said.

"You could advertise yourself as a clairvoyant. Actually, we'd prefer you call yourself a speaker. Regardless, the client comes to you and asks for the spirit they want to contact. We don't know whether you'll be able to hear the spirits directly, but if you can't, we can relay what they want to say. You pass that on to the client. They pay you, you pay your mortgage, you get to keep the house, and we get to live here with someone who can actually hear us. Everyone wins."

"That's ridiculous," I said. "I won't pretend to be like Mona."

"That's the whole point, Dorothy," Gray said. "You wouldn't be pretending. You'd be the real thing."

"You think these spirits are going to turn up just because I ask them to?"

"No." Bec's voice sounded like she was losing patience with

me. "They will come because the client asks for them. You will be the transponder."

"The what?"

"You pass on their message."

"It sounds ludicrous and it's probably illegal."

"What Mona is doing might be illegal, but you wouldn't be doing that," she said.

"I still think it's a bad idea."

"Worse than losing your house because you can't pay the mortgage?" she asked.

I sighed.

"Maybe you should just leave me alone for a while. I don't feel like talking about this right now."

Silence.

"Hello?" I asked. "Are you guys still here?"

No answer.

"You could have said goodbye."

I mulled over the spirits' proposal that evening as I flicked through the television channels. The pros were that it might actually give me a little income and I'd be able to work from home. The cons made a longer list, though. Advertising was expensive, most people would assume I was a fake, it was unsafe to have strangers coming into the house...

Actually, that was all I could come up with. Two pros and three cons. Not exactly a convincing argument. Well, I didn't have to give them a decision tonight. I could sleep on it.

I checked my emails as soon as I got up the next morning. Maybe I would have an interview request and I could forget about the whole crazy plan from the spirits. I did indeed have emails — seven more form rejections. I closed the laptop with a sigh.

"Spirits?" I asked. "Anyone there?"

"I'm here," Lissa said.

Her voice was always so eager. I got the feeling she badly wanted us to be friends. I supposed there weren't many opportunities to make new friends in the... whatever the place they were in was called.

"Have you made a decision?" Gray asked.

"Is everyone here?" I asked.

"We're all here," Bec said.

"I think we need some ground rules if we're going to live together," I said. "I don't like not knowing when you're here. So rule number one: You have to tell me when you arrive."

"Fair enough," Gray said.

"Rule number two: Stay out of the bathroom. I don't want to be wondering whether someone's watching every time I have a shower."

"That would only happen if we broke rule number one," Bec pointed out.

"Regardless," I said. "Rule number three: If I agree to this proposal of yours, it's a trial. If I change my mind, I don't want to hear about it forever."

"Fine," Bec said.

"Rule number four..." My voice trailed off. "Actually, I think that's all I have. Three rules."

"We have some rules too," Bec said. "Number one: You don't ask about our lives. Number two: You don't go poking around trying to figure out who we were or how we died. Number three: You don't tell anyone about us. Let them think you have some magical ability if that's what it takes, but we want to be anonymous. Number four: You will tell your clients only the truth and only so far as it won't be hurtful for them. Number five: If we say to stop with a client, you will do so immediately and without question. Number six: We don't do children. Number seven: If at any point we change our minds, it's over."

"That's more than twice as many rules as I have," I said.

"Do we have a deal, Dorothy?" she asked.

"What was the bit about children?"

"No children."

"Clients or spirits?" I asked.

"Clients. If an adult client seeks contact with a child spirit, we will help you because it might help the child. But we will not deal with child clients regardless of who they ask for."

"Okay. I suppose that all seems reasonable."

"Does that mean we have a deal?" Gray asked. "Are we going to do this?"

"I guess we are," I said. "We might really help people and not just the living ones, but the spirits, too."

"We're not in a movie." Bec's tone was prickly. "It's not all sweetness and light, just complete whatever your unfinished business is and zap, off you go to heaven. We don't know why we're here and we don't know whether we're supposed to go anywhere else."

I pretended to take her comments at face value.

"Maybe some spirits might be able to move on if they have the opportunity to say whatever it is they need to," I said. "Maybe some just need to see that the ones they've left behind are okay. It might even help you guys. Perhaps I can help you to... do whatever it is you need to do."

"Because obviously the spirits who are hanging around on the other side of the veil have unfinished business," Gray said.

"Rules number one and two," Bec said curtly.

I tried to remember which ones they were. No asking about their lives and no trying to figure out how they died. I think.

"What will we do if someone comes looking for one of you?" I asked. "A client, I mean."

"You will tell them you can't make contact and refund their money," Bec said. "Our lives are off limits. No exceptions."

"I guess I'll make a new ad then," I said.

TWELVE

An internet search revealed the concept of social media ads. I had never really used any kind of social media, and setting up my first ad turned out to be more complicated than I expected. However, I discovered that PPC, which some positions I had looked at required experience in, meant Pay Per Click ads. I could now honestly say I had created at least one PPC ad.

I watched my ads dashboard over the next couple of days, pleasantly surprised to find my ad was getting quite a lot of impressions, which meant people were actually seeing it, and even some clicks. Best of all, I could control the daily budget, so it wasn't costing more than I could afford.

My first client was a woman named Mrs Chapman. She was a little past middle-aged with immaculate make-up and grey hair cut into a sleek bob. She didn't blink when I asked for the hundred and fifty dollar fee upfront. Since my financial situation was so dire, I had decided to charge more than Mona.

I had learned a lot from my session with Mona. Prior to Mrs Chapman's arrival, I removed my old cracked sofa from the lounge room and replaced it with two wingback chairs that had sat in the spare room forever. They were threadbare, like everything I owned, but they didn't look too bad draped with a clean sheet. I positioned them so they faced each other, separated by a cheap coffee table I found at a secondhand store. On the coffee table sat two tea light candles. I didn't intend to light them for fear of burning down the house, but I figured they would be atmospheric anyway.

I had also bought some new clothes. Mona's appearance hadn't been at all what I expected so I channelled my inner bohemian. After spending a couple of hours traipsing around second-hand stores, I found a long skirt and a couple of flowy tops in dark shades of purple and blue. A choker on a black velvet band and a ring with a large grey moonstone completed my new look. I adjusted my glasses and wished I could get away without wearing them, but I didn't want to be squinting at my clients like Mona. Despite the glasses, I felt very new age and hoped it was what my clients would expect.

Mrs Chapman seemed to barely notice what I looked like. She positioned her not-inconsiderable behind on a chair, stuffed her handbag in between herself and the chair, and looked at me expectantly. As I sat across from her, an icy trickle of sweat started dripping between my shoulder blades. I was pretty sure I was about to make a monumental fool of myself.

"So, Mrs Chapman." I tried to sound warm and caring. "How can I help you today?"

"I want to contact Fifi," she said with the look that rich people give when they expect you to already know the minutiae of their lives.

I took a deep breath.

"And who is Fifi?"

"My poodle. She passed six months ago."

My heart was already pounding, but now it ratcheted up a level. I swallowed hard and tried to sound confident.

"Your poodle?"

"Fifi meant the world to me." Mrs Chapman's tone was already defensive. "She was my best friend, my constant companion, the only one who understood me."

I had no idea how to respond. It had never occurred to me that a client might want to speak with their poodle. Mrs Chapman had barely stopped talking before Gray spoke.

"Dorothy, this isn't going to work."

I didn't want Mrs Chapman to think I was odd, so I responded with a non-committal "oh?". Both she and Gray took that as a signal to continue. I tried to tune out her words in order to concentrate on his.

"There are no animals on this side of the veil," he said. "Even if there were, I doubt we could communicate with them in the way you need."

I restrained my groan. Of all the possible first clients, I had to have this one. She was still talking, something about fifteen wonderful years together.

"Mrs Chapman."

She closed her mouth with a snap and looked at me so hopefully that her fifties felt like they were burning right through the pocket in my skirt. I would have to refund her. There was no other ethical way to deal with the situation.

"Mrs Chapman, I'm very sorry, but I can't provide the contact you seek."

She looked at me blankly and shook her head. I tried not to stare at the way her jowls wobbled.

"Excuse me?" she said.

I took a deep breath and tried to steady myself. I needed her to see me as professional, but compassionate.

"Mrs Chapman, my spirit contacts tell me there are no animals in the place where they are. I can only conclude this means all animals cross over immediately, being much purer of heart than we humans are."

The words were out of my mouth before I thought them through and I cringed at their corniness.

Mrs Chapman continued to stare at me.

"Of course, I'll refund your money," I said.

Mrs Chapman raised one hand.

"Stop."

Her voice indicated she expected absolute obedience and I froze, my hand already halfway into my pocket.

"Are you telling me." Mrs Chapman carefully enunciated every word. She was making sure there was no miscommunication between us. "Are you telling me you cannot establish contact with my precious Fifi because there are no dogs in the other world?"

I nodded and tried not to gulp. I was determined to maintain a calm, professional appearance if it killed me.

"I'm so sorry, Mrs Chapman. I wish I could help you."

"And you are telling me that your spirit contacts say there are no animals at all in the place where they are?"

"That's correct."

I wanted to crawl away into a hole in the ground. So much for my new career.

"I have had sessions with four mediums since Fifi's passing. All four claimed to have made contact with her. If you are telling me the truth, then all four lied."

Oh, shit.

"Mrs Chapman—"

She stood, jowls wobbling, and I braced myself for the inevitable onslaught. But she leaned across the coffee table and snatched up my hand.

"Thank you." She squeezed my fingers so tightly I could

almost hear the bones grinding. "You have no idea what this means to me."

I was speechless, having expected a slap or a shake or worse. Instead, Mrs Chapman beamed at me.

"Dorothy, this is such a relief. You really are the real thing. All this time I've been trying to contact poor old Fifi, fighting to keep her with me, and now here you are, telling me she's already crossed over. My baby has moved on. That is the most reassuring thing you could tell any mother. All I want in the world is to know that Fifi — wherever she is — is well and happy, and you've given me more peace of mind than you could possibly imagine. So thank you."

It can be amazing how many words a person can get out before they have to stop for breath. As she ground the bones in my hand and blathered on about Fifi, I was still trying to retrieve her cash with my other hand.

"Your money, Mrs Chapman," I managed as she finally stopped for breath. "Of course I won't charge you for today. I'm terribly sorry I couldn't help you."

She shook her head and beamed at me.

"My dear, you misunderstand me. I am thrilled."

I couldn't think of anything to say.

"You have confirmed that my Fifi has crossed over. You cannot possibly imagine how good that makes me feel. I shall most certainly be recommending you to all my friends. Bless you, my dear. Bless you."

With that, Mrs Chapman released my hand, picked up her handbag and bustled out, leaving me staring open-mouthed at the door.

CHAPTER

THIRTEEN

"Well, that went well," Gray said. "I think."

"Way to go, Dorothy," Lissa said. "She loved you."

"And it sounds like you might get some referrals out of her." Bec, of course, was entirely practical.

I was still trying to figure out what had just happened.

"That wasn't so bad," I said, eventually. "Even if I couldn't give her what she wanted."

"Don't you see, Dorothy?" Grey asked. "You did give her what she wanted. You told her that Fifi has moved on."

I knew they each silently added, *unlike us*.

"She came here thinking she wanted to make contact," Gray said. "You gave her something more precious."

"We don't know whether Fifi has crossed over," Bec said. "We don't know what happens to the animals."

"That doesn't matter," Gray said. "Fifi isn't here and that's what the client wanted to hear."

Only two hours passed between Mrs Chapman's departure and the phone ringing. It rang and rang. It quickly became obvious I needed an appointment book of some sort. Trying to keep all the names and times straight in my phone calendar just wasn't cutting it. Every caller said Mrs Chapman had recommended me, and they all wanted an appointment as soon as possible.

I scheduled them for four a day, two in the morning and two in the afternoon. At a hundred and fifty dollars per client, that meant I'd be making six hundred dollars a day. Three thousand dollars a week. Even once I deducted income tax, I'd still be making almost triple what Mac used to pay me. I'd be able to cover the mortgage and pretty soon I'd even have enough money to replace the carpet and get a painter in like I had hoped. It was hard to believe.

The phone continued to ring and soon I was telling callers that I was fully booked for the next week. It didn't matter; they booked for the following week. The phone kept ringing and the bookings stretched forward for the next three weeks. The callers were no longer Mrs Chapman's friends; now they were friends of friends.

At ten p.m. I switched the phone to silent and let the calls go through to voicemail. I was exhausted. Only twelve hours had passed since Mrs Chapman's arrival and I now had more than eighty consultations booked. I hadn't eaten since breakfast, but I could barely summon the energy to open a bottle of wine, let alone cook something. Even the thought of microwaving a frozen meal was too much, so I made some toast.

I hadn't heard a peep out of the spirits for hours, but as I sat on a stool at the kitchen counter, I felt a strange shift in the air. A disturbance that felt like Gray. I was too tired to think about what this development meant. Right back at the start, before the spirits ever spoke to me, I had sometimes felt like someone else was in the room. But even once I knew about the spirits, I hadn't been able to identify who was there with me.

"Gray." I greeted him with my raised wine glass. "I really hope I don't screw this up."

My toast was going cold, but it seemed like too much effort to pick it up. And if I picked it up, I'd have to chew it, which would be even more effort.

"Just remember we're doing this to help," he said. "We're helping you to keep the house, and you're helping your clients to get some measure of peace. If you keep that in the forefront of your mind, it will all work out."

"That sounds very wise."

"Of course I'm wise. I think it's a mandatory requirement for a spirit."

Another gulp of wine and I felt better. I might even find the energy to deal with that toast soon. In my semi-drunken state, my mouth became a little loose.

"What do you remember, Gray?"

A stony silence.

"I've told you before to leave it alone." The words were short and his tone snappy.

"I just—"

"Drop it, Dorothy. If you want my help, you'll leave it alone."

He left.

Why did I say that? I knew he didn't want to talk about his past, and yet I kept asking, despite Bec's rules. I staggered over to the sink and poured the rest of the wine out before tossing the toast in the bin.

"This is why I don't drink," I muttered as I rinsed the glistening red drops from the sink. "Alcohol makes you do stupid things."

"Dorothy, are you okay?" Lissa asked.

In my distraction, I hadn't noticed her arrival. Or perhaps I couldn't feel her the way I had felt Gray.

"I'm fine," I snapped.

"Did you and Gray have a fight? He's real mad about something."

"You wouldn't understand."

"You want me to tell him you're sorry?"

I sighed, my annoyance evaporating. She was only trying to help.

"No, Lissa, I don't want you to tell him anything."

"But what happened? I thought you and Gray were friends."

"You're too young to understand." The words were out of my mouth before I thought about it.

There was a choked sob and when Lissa spoke, her voice was teary.

"That was mean, Dorothy."

Then she was gone.

"Lissa, wait."

She didn't come back.

"Dorothy, what is going on with you tonight?" It was Bec's turn now. "Gray is in a right funk and now you've upset Lissa as well."

"I know. I'm sorry."

I leaned against the kitchen counter, wishing I hadn't drunk so much on an empty stomach. My head spun and my belly was no happier with me than the spirits.

"You'd better find a way to make it up to both of them," Bec said. "You need us."

I stumbled up to my bedroom and fell into bed without bothering to change into my pyjamas. Had I made a huge mistake? Perhaps it would have been wiser to keep looking for a regular job.

I slept restlessly, my dreams interspersed with guilt over upsetting both Gray and Lissa, and panic at the mayhem Mrs

Chapman's appointment had created. At some point, I got up long enough to undress and crawl in under the covers.

The sun's first rays were already brightening the room when I next woke. I could feel that Lissa was there, although she didn't speak.

"I'm sorry, Lissa," I said. "Really."

"It's okay. I know you were upset about Gray. You didn't mean what you said, did you?"

It was more a hopeful query than a statement of fact.

"Of course I didn't. I was upset, but I shouldn't have taken it out on you."

"I forgive you. Because that's what friends do, isn't it? They fight, but then they make up and forgive each other. So this means we're friends, doesn't it?"

"Of course we are, Lissa."

"It's nice to have a friend." Her voice was wistful now. "I don't think I've ever had a real friend before, but now I've got you. Samson says he's my friend, too."

That was something I could relate to. Being a teenager with no friends.

"What about Bec and Gray?" I asked. "Aren't they your friends too?"

Lissa hesitated. "Sort of. But they're different."

"What do you mean?"

"Bec is all bossy and mothering. She looks after me, but it's like she does it because she has to. And Gray... he's just Gray."

I wasn't sure I understood, but was learning to leave well enough alone.

"Well, you and I are friends at any rate." I forced a note of cheeriness into my voice as I dragged myself out of bed and pulled on a dressing gown. My head pounded and I really needed a shower. "I could do with a friend right now."

"Why, Dorothy? Are you sad?"

"Not sad. More worried."

"About your appointments?"

"Mm."

Better that she thought that was all. There had to be a reason I could suddenly communicate with these four spirits, but what was it? I've never been one to believe in fate or destiny or whatever label you want to put on it, but I sure as hell didn't believe in coincidence either. That might sound like a contradiction, but my gut told me that this situation was no coincidence. I was meant to do something.

Or maybe the spirits themselves were supposed to do something. Maybe they weren't what they seemed to be. Maybe it was all a pretence to get me to help them with something they couldn't do alone. My thoughts got too tangled when I tried to think about it.

Why these particular spirits? Bec, Lissa and Samson seemed to have a connection to the house. Presumably, they had all lived here at some point. Maybe Gray had too, but it was his connection to me that bothered me the most. Was there any possibility he was my brother? Surely I would recognise Gary, even if I couldn't see him. His name was strangely close to Gray, but Gray had said he thought he was military, which Gary definitely was not.

So if Gray wasn't Gary, who was he? I didn't have any long-lost lovers who might be hanging around for last words with me, despite Mona's conviction, and there were no close friends who had died. I had never had much contact with my extended family. There were a few aunts and uncles out there, but I had no idea whether any of them had died. Could Gray be one of them? Maybe even one of my grandfathers?

It probably wouldn't take a lot of effort to find out a bit

about the three spirits who had lived in my house. But I had promised I wouldn't try to look into their lives and if I broke Bec's rules again, they might withdraw their help. I would lose the house if that happened. Also, I wasn't sure I wanted to know. What if I discovered my house had a bloody past full of tragic deaths? How could I sleep there at night if I knew? Gray was the one I wanted to know about anyway, and I didn't have enough information to find out anything about him. Lissa's voice broke into my reverie.

"Dorothy? You okay?"

I must have been standing there, staring into space with my hands still in the act of wrapping the cord of my dressing gown around my waist.

"Sorry, just thinking. Come on. I need some coffee."

Bec arrived as I was boiling the water.

"Good morning," I said.

"Are we in a better mood today?" Her tone was snappy. Lissa may have forgiven me, but Bec obviously hadn't.

"I am, thank you."

I had already made up with Lissa and I'd apologise to Gray when he turned up. Bec could sulk about me offending her little brood if she wanted, but I darned well wouldn't apologise to her as well.

Bec harrumphed, but I concentrated on making my coffee and pretended I hadn't heard. I sat at the kitchen counter and sorted through the scraps of paper I had written my appointments on, trying to make sure I had transferred them all into my phone calendar. I tuned out a whispered conversation between Bec and Lissa.

"What time is your first consultation this morning?" Bec sounded calmer now. Whatever Lissa said hadn't completely mollified her, but at least she was attempting to be pleasant.

"Nine thirty and the next is at eleven."

"Well, good luck with those." Bec's presence faded.

"Whoah, wait a minute, Bec. You're not leaving, are you?"

"I assumed my presence wasn't required. Gray can handle most of it."

"What if Gray needs help?" I asked.

"There's Samson, and even Lissa."

I took a deep breath. I couldn't afford to have Bec mad at me. She seemed to be the leader of this little group of spirits. How long would the others help me without her?

"Bec, I need your ability to make everyone feel like they're part of a team. I'm not real good at that."

Bec sniffed — her *I'm not impressed* sniff — but I sensed she was pleased.

"No, you're not."

I got up to make another coffee. My one-coffee-a-day rule had gone out the window along with my job.

"Let's go over the plan once more," I said. "The clients will ask for a particular spirit and one of you will let me know whether the spirit is here, right? I assume you're counting on the spirit coming with the client?"

I felt Gray's presence arrive.

"Not exactly," he said.

"Good morning, Gray," I said. "Is Samson here too?"

"Not yet," Bec said. "He will be, though."

"Gray, what did you mean by not exactly?" I asked.

"We haven't done this before," he said. "But we think that sometimes the spirit will travel with the client."

"Like Gray does with you," Lissa interjected.

"But otherwise we suspect that if the client asks for a particular spirit, they will essentially summon them. The client calls the spirit and the spirit comes."

"You suspect? That doesn't sound very definite. I thought you were sure about this."

"We have no way of knowing until you try," Bec said. "We can only tell you what we have observed ourselves."

"And I'll be able to talk directly to the spirit?"

"Maybe," Gray said. "If you can't communicate with them, one of us will act as a medium."

It hadn't sounded this complicated before, although now that I thought about it, I couldn't remember whether I had been sober the last time we discussed the plan.

"You should get dressed," Bec said. "It's almost a quarter to nine and you don't want to be wandering around in your dressing gown if the client turns up early."

"Good idea."

I hadn't eaten, but my stomach rolled at the thought.

"Tonight, right after your last appointment, you need to go buy a diary," Bec said. "Preferably one that shows a week at a time. Put all of your appointments in it and then leave it open so I can keep an eye on it. We don't have any sense of time here, but if you write the times clearly and legibly, I can watch the kitchen clock and try to keep track of them."

"Thanks, Bec. I'd really appreciate that."

Bec sniffed again and I realised I had misinterpreted the sound previously. It didn't just mean *I'm not impressed* but also *I'm pleased*. I felt like I'd made a breakthrough in understanding her.

"Go straight after your last appointment," she said. "Now, go get dressed."

As I left, Bec was busy bossing Gray and Lissa.

I showered and dressed in my new skirt and top. I brushed my hair and added a pair of pearl earrings my parents had given me for my fifteenth birthday. Then I fastened the velvet choker around my neck. I examined myself in the mirror and took off the pearls. They didn't fit with the new age image I was going for.

74

I didn't want a grumbling tummy distracting me during a consultation, so I ate a piece of toast while leaning over the kitchen sink so I didn't drop crumbs all down my front. A quick brush of my teeth and I was ready. There was nothing left to do but wait for my second client to arrive.

FOURTEEN

At precisely nine twenty-five, the doorbell rang. The thin, nervous-looking woman outside jumped as I opened the door.

"Are you Dorothy?" she asked before I could say anything.

"Yes, I am. You must be Mrs Wright. Please come in."

I was aiming for confident and professional, and I thought I pulled it off.

Mrs Wright slid through the doorway, ever so careful not to touch either me or the door, and perched on the edge of a wingback.

"Margo Chapman recommended you." Her gaze darted around the room. "She said you're very good. I do hope you can help me."

"I'll do my best." I gave her what I hoped would be a soothing smile. "Why don't you tell me who you want to contact?"

"Jennifer May Wright." She clutched her handbag to her chest. "My daughter."

I kept my face fixed in a neutral expression despite the

sinking feeling in my gut. "And how old was Jennifer when she passed?"

"Four years, seven months and two days."

Composure, that's what I needed. Of all the potential clients I could have, a grieving mother surely had to be the worst. I closed my eyes, so I wouldn't have to look at Mrs Wright, and took a deep breath to steady my nerves.

"Speak to me, spirits," I said, which was our signal that I was ready to begin. We had agreed I would repeat the name and age of the spirit in question, to give my contacts a little time. They didn't know whether they might need to coax the summoned spirit to speak. "I seek contact with Jennifer May Wright, aged four."

"Four years, seven months," Mrs Wright added. "And two days."

Her voice trailed off. I kept my eyes closed, not wanting to see her face.

"Just a minute, Dorothy."

Gray's voice sounded strained. Did he have children of his own once?

"We have her here," he said. "She says her mother looks older than she remembers."

I could have sighed with relief.

"Mrs Wright, Jennifer says you look older. How long has it been?"

"Six years, nine—" She cut herself off. "Almost seven years. Are you sure it is her? Is there a way you can prove it? I don't mean any disrespect, but..."

"No offence taken, Mrs Wright. Spirits, can you ask Jennifer to tell me something that only she and her mother would know?"

There was only a brief pause before Gray spoke. I relayed his words to Mrs Wright.

"She remembers a toy rabbit. It had long floppy ears, a purple ribbon and no tail."

There was a loud sob and, against my better judgement, I opened my eyes. Mrs Wright hunched over, sobbing into her handbag.

"Mrs Wright? Are you okay?"

"Yes, yes," she said between sobs.

"Do you remember the rabbit?"

She opened her handbag and retrieved a tattered bunny wearing a faded purple ribbon around its neck. I didn't need to see its back to know there would be no tail.

"Oh my god, I can't believe it," Mrs Wright said between sobs. "It's Jennifer. You're really talking to her."

"I don't mean to hurry you, Mrs Wright, but I don't know how long I will have access to Jennifer. Is there something you would like to tell her?"

She started choking down her sobs and I looked away while she composed herself. A large wad of tissues came out of her handbag and I made a mental note to put a box of tissues on the coffee table. Perhaps a glass of water would also be appropriate.

"Could you..." A pause before she was able to continue. "Could you tell her I love her and I miss her. I count every day that we're apart and I am so, so sorry. I only left her for a moment. Just a few seconds while I went to answer the phone. When I came back, she was floating, face down. I jumped in and grabbed her, but she was already—" Mrs Wright broke down again.

I waited a moment before I spoke, wanting to be sure I could trust my voice. Later, after Mrs Wright left, I knew I would shed a few private tears for poor drowned Jennifer.

"Spirits, can you hear Mrs Wright?"

"We heard her, Dorothy. Give us a second. We've got tears on our side, too."

"Just a moment, Mrs Wright. Jennifer..." I hesitated, wondering how much to tell her.

"Is she still there? Has she gone already?"

"It's all right. She's still there. She's just a little teary."

Mrs Wright straightened her back and started dabbing her eyes dry.

"Oh my god, I didn't think of that. Jenny, baby, Mamma's so sorry to have upset you."

Gray relayed Jennifer's words.

"Mrs Wright, Jennifer asks if you remember the day you went to the park and she played with the white puppy? She says it had a red collar and it licked her right on the mouth."

Mrs Wright muffled another sob. "Jenny, that's a lovely memory. We had such a good time that day."

"She says you went past an ice-cream van and she begged to have one. You never let her eat junk food and that was her first ice cream. She had a chocolate cone and she says it was the nicest thing she ever ate."

Gray interrupted with a clarification.

"I'm sorry. She says I got that wrong. The chocolate cone was the very nicest thing she ever ate."

Mrs Wright swallowed hard.

"That was what she always used to say, right from when she could speak. If she liked something, it was always the very nicest thing."

"You told her it wasn't proper to speak like that, but she would get excited and forget what she was supposed to say."

"Yes, I always corrected her, but she persisted in saying it. Jenny, baby..." Mrs Wright hesitated. "Are you okay where you are?"

"She's fine. There are other children there and also a very nice young man called Dan who looks after her. Apparently she reminds him of someone he left behind."

I fought to keep my voice steady. I wasn't prepared for this. Hadn't expected to feel so emotional.

Mrs Wright was trying hard to appear composed, although not very successfully. Gray spoke quickly now. Jennifer was going back to wherever Mrs Wright had summoned her from.

"Mrs Wright, I'm losing contact with Jennifer. She says she loves you and she misses you and that you were the very nicest mother she could have had."

"Goodbye, Jenny baby," Mrs Wright said, blinking very fast. "I love you, sweetheart."

"I'm sorry, Mrs Wright. My spirit contact tells me she's gone. She can't see or hear you anymore."

She cried in earnest then. I went into the kitchen for a few minutes to give her some privacy. She was just pulling herself back together when I returned.

"Thank you, thank you so much." Mrs Wright grabbed my hand and squeezed it hard. "I can't tell you how much this means to me. Margot Chapman was right. You really are the real thing."

Mrs Wright fished in her handbag and pulled out a handful of cash. She crushed it into my hand.

"Here, please take it. I'd give you more if I could, but this is all I have on me. Thank you again."

She left, although it was a long time before she drove away. I felt sorry for her, sitting in her car in front of a stranger's house, sobbing because she had just spoken to her drowned daughter.

I didn't look at the money until after she had gone. It didn't matter if she hadn't paid the full amount. I'd be happy with whatever she could afford. I had given her something impor-tant and that mattered more than money. When I did count it, I was stunned. Almost three hundred dollars. Double my fee.

Between this and Mrs Chapman's money, I already had a quarter of my monthly mortgage payment.

I cried for a while after she drove away. I've never had children, never even wanted them, but I felt deeply affected by my time with Mrs Wright and little Jennifer. The spirits were silent while I cried until Bec pointed out that the next client was due in less than half an hour.

CHAPTER

FIFTEEN

T he rest of the day was a blur. My eleven a.m. appointment was an elderly woman seeking contact with her twin sister, who had died at twenty. After lunch, there was a middle-aged woman who wanted to speak with her husband who had passed six months ago.

Both consultations went well, much to my surprise. The spirits my clients asked for came. I couldn't hear either of them myself, so Bec acted as the intermediary for the twin sister, and Gray handled my third client's husband. Neither of those consultations distressed me the way Mrs Wright's had, but they were still full of tension and emotion, and it surprised me how exhausted I was after. Thankfully I had only scheduled four appointments a day.

My last consultation on that first day was a middle-aged woman who fiddled with a ring on her finger. Mrs Williams sat right on the very edge of the chair. I wasn't sure whether it was because she didn't want to crease her skirt, which looked expensive, or whether she thought my chair would be dirty. I made a mental note to wash the sheet I had draped over it.

"Who would you like to make contact with, Mrs Williams?"

I felt like I was hitting my stride. The patter came easier with each client and my confidence grew.

"My son," she whispered. "Damian Williams."

"And how old was Damian when he passed?"

"Twenty-nine."

I closed my eyes.

"Speak to me, spirits. I'm seeking contact with Damian Williams, aged twenty-nine."

A long silence. When Gray finally spoke, he sounded harried.

"Give us another minute, Dorothy."

"My spirit contacts advise me they are trying to locate your son," I said to Mrs Williams.

Several minutes passed, each feeling like an hour.

"Dorothy, we have a problem," Gray said.

It was difficult to ask for details without alerting Mrs Williams.

"Tell me."

"He isn't here," Gray said.

That would teach me to get cocky. I kept my eyes closed as I took a deep breath. I didn't want to look at Mrs Williams. Didn't want to see the devastation on her face when I told her I couldn't provide the contact she wanted.

"Are you sure?" I asked.

"I'm sorry."

"Could you clarify that?"

"I don't know how else to say it, Dorothy. He's not here."

There was no way I could continue this conversation without Mrs Williams knowing what was wrong, but there was nothing else for it.

"Is he not there or just not answering?" I asked.

I could hear the way her breathing changed. She knew. Oh dear lord, I didn't want to do this.

"It's odd." Gray sounded puzzled. "He just isn't here. I don't know how else to explain it. Each of the other spirits has come when your client said their name. It's like they summoned the spirit and they can't *not* come. But Damien didn't. We've tried calling him ourselves and there's no answer."

I took another deep breath and opened my eyes. Mrs Williams' face was pale and hopeful.

"Mrs Williams. I'm very sorry, but my spirit contacts are unable to find Damian."

The hope in her face increased, and I realised why she was so hopeful.

"Mrs Williams, are you sure Damian has passed?"

A tear escaped her eye and she smiled. A very small, very sad smile.

"No," she said. "I'm not sure at all. I haven't heard from him for almost fifteen years. He walked out one day and never came back. I've always believed he was alive. That he was still out there somewhere. I thought I would know if he had died."

"I don't understand, Mrs Williams. Why did you come to me if you were so sure he was alive?"

More tears trickled down her cheeks as she smiled.

"Margot Chapman told me what happened when she asked to speak with Fifi. She said you wouldn't lie to me. That if you couldn't find him, he was alive."

Mrs Williams stood and pressed some cash into my hand. She closed the door quietly behind her as she left. I just sat there, confused.

"Well done, Dorothy," Lissa said.

I felt the spirits gather around me like a blanket. For a moment, I could even sense Samson. Their presence was warm and comforting.

"Thank you," I said. "I couldn't have done this today without you."

"Of course you couldn't," Bec said.

"You're welcome, Dorothy," Lissa said. "It's nice to feel useful."

There was no time to sit back and reflect on my day before Bec hurried me off to buy a diary.

"Make sure it's one of those big ones," she called as I left. "A week to a double page."

The newsagent was only a ten-minute walk away and I was thankful for the time to think. I wasn't far from home when Gray joined me. He didn't speak, but seemed content to accompany me in silence. That suited me just fine.

At the newsagent, I rummaged through a bin of marked-down diaries and finally found one which fitted Bec's requirements. Paper bag in hand, I set off for home again. We were almost there before Gray spoke.

"You did good today."

"It was all of us. We're a team."

"Mm."

"Gray, can I ask you something?"

He was silent. Since he hadn't said no, I pressed on.

"Why do they remember more than you?"

"What do you mean?" he asked.

"You told me that none of you remember much, but the spirits we contacted today had extensive memories. Very detailed ones. Why don't you guys remember like that?"

"Rule number one, Dorothy."

I felt his presence disappear. I had broken one of their rules by asking about his life. It made no sense for the four spirits who inhabited my house to be the only ones who remembered so little. They were pretending not to remember. The thing I didn't understand was why.

SIXTEEN

I had scheduled my first appointment each day for nine thirty a.m. So on Monday, I planned to sleep in. After ten years of leaving home at eight, sleeping in on a weekday felt almost indecent. When the phone rang, it dragged me most reluctantly from a deep sleep. I picked up my mobile and mumbled something I hoped would pass for hello.

"Why, good morning," a chirpy voice said. "I do hope I haven't woken you."

"Eh?" I squinted at the bedside clock. I'm as blind as a bat without my glasses, but it looked like seven fifteen. That woke me up a little. Who on earth would ring so early?

"I've heard about the seances you've been conducting and I'd like to make an urgent appointment."

I fumbled for my glasses and switched my phone to speaker so I could check my online calendar.

"I'm booked out for a few weeks, but let me check when I'm available."

"I do hope you can do something very quickly," she said. "It's terribly urgent."

"April second is the first time I have free."

"Oh, no, that is far too long." Her voice sounded like she was pouting. How did she do that? "I need something much sooner. Can't you squeeze me in today?"

"I'm sorry, April second is the earliest I can do."

"Oh, but I really need an urgent appointment."

"Would you like to book for the second?" I asked.

She sighed dramatically, but didn't answer my question. I said nothing while I waited. I would have to be firm with people like this. Four appointments a day was exhausting enough, given how emotional each session was. I didn't want to be squeezing in extras just because someone said it was urgent.

"No, I guess I'll book with someone else," she said at last, her voice dripping with disappointment.

"Okay. I'm sorry I couldn't help you."

I quickly hung up before she could press me any further. As I got out of the shower the phone rang again. I wrapped a towel around myself and tried not to notice how much water I dripped across the carpet as I dashed back into the bedroom.

"Ms Marks, this is Lola James from *The Brisbane Journal*. I wondered if I could make a time to interview you?"

"Interview me?"

"Yes, I heard about you from Margot Chapman and my paper would like to run a story on you."

Her voice was awfully familiar.

"Did you ring earlier to make an appointment?" I asked.

Her laugh sounded false.

"Why, no, I've just arrived at work a few minutes ago and you're the first thing on my list for today. The most important thing. I can be at your house in an hour if that would suit you."

"I have a client in an hour and I'm busy all day. Let me check my calendar."

I was tempted to remind her I had already told her I was booked until April second. But an interview would be good publicity and it was free. I flicked through the next couple of days in my calendar app. Lola tapped something against her phone. The noise distracted me and I couldn't think clearly. For some reason, my first appointment on Friday wasn't until ten thirty, but with Lola's tapping, I couldn't remember why it was so late. Would it give me enough time for an interview?

"I have some time on Friday if you could be here by eight-thirty."

"Oh, couldn't we meet earlier than that?" she asked. "I have a deadline at four p.m. and I was really hoping to have this story in by then. That would mean we'd make it into tomorrow's paper."

It was definitely her that rang earlier. No wonder she wanted an urgent appointment.

"I'm sorry. I'm fully booked with clients. I just happen to have a later appointment on Friday morning. Otherwise, the next time I have any availability is April second."

Like I told you earlier.

"What about tomorrow morning? My editor is super-interested in this story, but I guess I could persuade him to hold it over until tomorrow and we'd make Wednesday's edition."

"I'm sorry, um..." Mental blank.

"Lola," she supplied helpfully. "Lola James, *The Brisbane Journal.*"

"Lola. I'm sorry, but it's either Friday or April second."

"Oh, gee whiz, I don't know if my editor will still be interested by then."

Was she playing games with me? Was I supposed to beg for her time and quickly change my appointments? I would have to toughen up if I wanted to get off the phone.

"Sorry, Lola. I can book you in for Friday or we can leave it and see what your editor wants. But if someone else books that time, April second will be the earliest I can do."

"I'll take it. Eight-thirty, you said?"

"That's right. I'll see you then."

I hung up before she could say anything else.

"Smooth," Gray said.

I hadn't noticed his arrival. I thought he was joking.

"Why does she want to interview me?"

"I guess you've made some waves."

"Me?"

Ordinary, almost-middle-aged me? Me who had been fired six weeks ago? Okay, I had managed to communicate with a couple of spirits, thanks to my friends beyond the veil, but I'd also had two consultations where I had utterly failed. Remember Fifi the poodle? And poor Mrs James, whose son I wasn't able to contact. She took that as confirmation that he was still alive. Me, I was never really sure. Perhaps he simply chose not to answer her call. He must have cut off contact with his mother for a reason. I could relate to that.

"Running a little late this morning, are we?" Bec asked as I made some coffee. She sounded typically bossy and un-cheery.

I glanced at the clock. Eight forty. I must have misread the time earlier.

"Crap."

I tossed some bread into the toaster. No time for the grilled ham and tomatoes I had intended to make.

"If we're going to do this, Dorothy, we are going to do it properly," Bec said as I splashed hot water into my mug and burnt my mouth trying to gulp it down before it had cooled. "I want you ready by nine o'clock every morning. That means you've showered, eaten and done whatever it is you spend half the morning waffling around doing."

I didn't have time to be offended or to even wonder what she was talking about.

"Sure, Bec."

"At nine a.m., you will switch your mobile to silent."

"Okay." I buttered a slice of toast and ate it in four bites.

"Then you will be ready and waiting in case your first client is early. It is not a good look to not be ready, even if the client is early."

"Whatever you say, Bec."

"Dorothy, are you taking this seriously?"

I paused, a second slice of toast midway to my mouth.

"Of course I am. Have you forgotten I'm unemployed? Have you noticed that the country seems to be slipping into a recession and there aren't a lot of jobs available? Have you realised that I don't have many options other than to make this work? These clients will be paying my mortgage. You bet I'm taking it seriously."

"Good." She sounded somewhat mollified. "You should."

"I am."

My irritation rose and I took a deep breath. With a client due in less than an hour, I couldn't afford to offend her. Bec seemed to be the glue holding my little posse of spirits together. I didn't know what would happen without her.

"Fine," she said. "Now I assume you won't be taking appointments over the weekends?"

"Not unless I have to."

"Okay then, on Friday evening, after your last appointment for the day, you will turn the page in your diary so I can see your appointments for the next week."

"Do you think you can turn the page yourself?"

I knew instantly I had said the wrong thing. Bec huffed and I felt her presence fade.

"Bec, don't go. I'm sorry. I didn't mean it the way it sounded."

Her presence grew stronger.

"What I meant was, have you ever tried to do it? To move something? A page is very light. I wonder if you could."

"You think I haven't tried?" She sounded tired.

"Have you?"

"We all have. None of us can move anything. It doesn't matter what it is or how light. Even collectively, we have no impact on anything in the physical world."

"Oh. I'm sorry. I'll make sure I turn the page on Friday evening."

"Good. Because I can only help you be organised if I can see your appointments."

I restrained myself from asking what difference it made. After all, it wasn't like I asked my clients who they wanted to contact or what relationship they had with the deceased, so there was nothing Bec could actually do to prepare. All my diary showed was a time, a name and a phone number. But if this let Bec feel useful, I wouldn't quibble.

CHAPTER
SEVENTEEN

I was so busy with my new schedule that exhaustion was hitting me hard and by Friday I could barely drag myself out of bed when the alarm went off. I shrugged on my dressing gown and went to make a coffee. Bec arrived while I was waiting for the water to boil.

"Good morning, Dorothy," she said. "What day is it today?"

"Friday. Or at least I hope it is. I really need a weekend."

"If that's the case, you have Lola James coming this morning. Eight-thirty."

"Eight-thirty?" I yawned and leaned against the kitchen counter, wishing the water would hurry and boil already. "Why did I schedule her so early?"

"Lola James is the journalist." Bec made a noise that sounded suspiciously like an exasperated sigh.

"Huh?" The water was finally ready and I filled my mug, then sat on a bar stool. For a moment, I closed my eyes. I had almost forgotten Bec and she huffed to remind me. I opened my eyes and sat up straighter. "What? You said something about a journalist."

"Lola James, the journalist from *The Brisbane Journal*. Remember? She's coming to interview you."

"Oh, crap." I set the mug down on the counter a little too hard and coffee sloshed out, burning my hand. "Damn it."

The spilled coffee had cooled by the time I found a cloth that was both dry and also clean enough to use on the kitchen counter. I wiped up the mess and tossed the cloth in the sink. The coffee in my mug was also too cold by then, so I tipped it out and made a new one. Coffee should be drunk black and extremely hot. It's the only way.

"So, what do you plan to say to her?" I had forgotten Bec again and she was making a weird little humming sound that I guessed signalled extreme impatience.

"Who?"

She huffed again.

"Dorothy, I'm trying very hard to help you, but you're not making it easy. Can you please focus for two minutes?"

I took a small, scalding sip of coffee and set the mug down.

"Sorry, Bec. I'm listening."

She didn't respond and I restrained a sigh. I couldn't afford to upset her before my day's consultations. Once Bec got worked up about something, it could take ages to placate her. She hadn't left, though. I could feel her there, waiting for me to cajole her.

"I'm sorry." I tried to make my voice sound sincere, although, truth be told, I wasn't sure what I had done wrong. "You know I need your help with this. What do I need to know about my appointment this morning?"

Bec let the silence stretch out for another few moments, then huffed again.

"I'm only trying to help."

"I know and I'm sorry I wasn't listening. I wasn't quite awake yet."

"Well then, if you're sure you're ready to work now?"

"I am, Bec. I'm sorry."

Sheesh, she was hard work for a dead woman.

"You have Lola James, the journalist from *The Brisbane Journal* coming this morning. I think we need to talk about what you're going to say to her."

"Oh, I remember now. I guess she'll have some questions, so I'll just try to answer them."

"I think we can make a pretty good guess at what she's going to ask." Bec sounded miffed again, although I had no idea what I'd done this time. "You've obviously created something of a sensation."

"A sensation? Bec, don't you think that's exaggerating a bit?"

"Have you forgotten that you've got four appointments a day booked for the next I-don't-know-how-many weeks? Clearly, Mrs Chapman went home and rang everyone she knows to tell them about her fabulous new psychic."

It surprised me to hear Bec use such a word. I would have expected psychic to be considered a dirty word, given her previous comments about clairvoyants. I had become so used to thinking of myself as a speaker that psychic grated uncomfortably.

"Please don't call me that. That's what you would call someone who pretends they can speak to spirits. Like people who contact the police claiming they know where a body is buried. I'm not one of those."

"That's exactly my point." Bec sounded more patient now. Perhaps she had been testing me. "You need to think about how you're going to answer questions about your ability."

"What should I say? I'll sound like I'm nuts if I tell her it just suddenly happened."

"I agree."

"Great." I tried not to sound too sarcastic. "What do you recommend I say?"

"That you've always been able to communicate with spirits."

"But that's not true."

"She's a journalist, Dorothy. She's not interested in the truth."

"She's not?"

"Of course not. She's interested in what will make the best story. So you tell her you've always been able to communicate with spirits and that for the last few months you've felt a calling in this direction. An urge to use your ability to help people. Then you were made redundant and you realised the universe was taking action to force you to listen since you were ignoring its hints."

While Bec was speaking, I felt Gray arrive. I was still trying to figure out how to tactfully tell Bec that her story sounded like a load of crap when he spoke up.

"Bec, are you sure that's wise?" he asked.

"Lola is looking for a good story," she said. "So we give her one. The more publicity Dorothy gets, the more clients she'll attract."

"Yes, but the story you've created doesn't sound like Dorothy at all." Good thing he was the one saying this. He was far more tactful than I would have been. "Maybe now that you've given her a framework to use, Dorothy should think about how to put it into her own words."

I could have kissed him.

"I think that sounds like a good idea," I said before Bec could argue. "In fact, I'm off to have a shower now and think about what to say. Thanks for your help, Bec."

I made it out of the kitchen before they started arguing.

CHAPTER

EIGHTEEN

The doorbell rang twenty-five minutes before Lola James was due. Thank goodness for Bec's insistence that I was always ready early. I opened the door to a woman who was short, curvy, and bouncy. Blond ringlets framed her face and she had large, suspiciously perky breasts. I stared — at the ringlets, not the breasts — wondering how on earth she got her hair to do that. She stuck out her hand, shoving it almost in my face.

"Lola James," she said. "*The Brisbane Journal.* Are you Dorothy?"

"Ah, um, yes."

Great start. I already felt like a fool. It doesn't matter how old you are, that sort of woman always makes you feel like a ten-year-old.

"It's so nice to meet you, Dorothy." Lola presented me with a wide smile which displayed her impeccably white, straight teeth. "May I come in?"

And there I was, feeling like an idiot again.

"Of course."

I stepped aside and she was in the door before I could

change my mind. I guessed she couldn't afford for people to have second thoughts and decide they didn't want her in their home. Without waiting for any further invitation, Lola settled herself on a chair and looked around the room with curiosity. I flushed a little. She probably didn't live in an old house that needed painting and new carpet.

"Is this where you do your séances?" Lola flashed me another perfect smile as she whipped a notebook and a voice recorder out of her handbag. She clicked the recorder on and sat it on the coffee table between us.

"They're not séances," I said before I could stop myself.

Lola stared at me with a look that suggested she was holding her breath as she waited for me to continue. Did she practise that look in the mirror?

"They're not séances."

And again, I felt like an idiot. Geez, why did these perfect-looking women have such power over us mere ordinary folk?

"Yes, I contact the dead, but I do it with respect for both the living and the dead. I'm not sitting in the dark, making my clients jump at spooky noises."

Lola raised a perfectly plucked eyebrow.

"Well, let's start at the beginning then, shall we, Dorothy? How long have you had this ability to... contact the dead?"

I wondered whether she paused for emphasis or was trying to avoid *I see dead people* connotations.

"I came to a gradual realisation of my ability over some time." Like a few weeks.

"And how long have you been doing this professionally?"

"This is my second week. I've wanted to use my ability to communicate with the spirits to help people for almost as long as I knew I could do this. When I lost my job, I thought that maybe someone was trying to tell me it was time for a career change. So I advertised online and started getting some clients.

It's gone crazy since then. I'm booked out for weeks at the moment."

"Margot Chapman is a family friend," Lola said. "She told me about how she came to you to make contact with her poodle." She paused to check her notebook. "Fifi."

She looked up at me and waited. I guessed I was meant to infer a question from that.

"Mrs Chapman was my first client. Unfortunately, I wasn't able to contact Fifi for her."

"And yet she was thrilled with the service you provided."

Lola was quite right in pointing out the contradiction, but I didn't know how to explain. I must have spent too long thinking because she moved right on.

"Margot told me she had been to numerous psychics—"

"Speakers," I interjected.

"Before contacting you and they had all claimed to have made contact with Fifi. They said things like how much Fifi missed her and loved her, but Margot was dissatisfied with that. She told me she couldn't *feel* Fifi anywhere and she was sure that if Fifi was *there* somewhere, she would be able to feel her. So she consulted psychic after psychic—"

"Speaker."

"Hoping eventually someone would be able to confirm Fifi had crossed over, which of course is what Margot believed had already happened."

She stopped talking and looked at me expectantly.

"I see." I didn't see anything. None of this was news to me.

"And then she found you."

"Yes, she did."

"And you were able to tell her that Fifi had crossed over."

I hesitated. I could see how this conversation would play out if I tried to correct her. No matter what I said, it would come out wrong, and Mrs Chapman was likely to read this article. She was probably responsible for at least ninety-five per cent of my bookings.

"Yes, I did."

May I burn in hell forever. Or linger on the other side of the veil. Whichever is the least worse.

"And you offered her a refund."

"I did. It didn't seem right to keep her money when I couldn't facilitate the contact she wanted."

Lola tilted her head and arranged her face in an expression of serious consideration.

"I see."

No question there. I waited.

The silence stretched. Was this a technique to make me feel uncomfortable and rush in to fill the silence? I forced myself to keep my mouth shut and looked down at my clenched hands. Despite my determination to wait her out, I was almost at breaking point before Lola stirred.

"I see." She glanced down at her notebook and flashed me that straight-teeth smile again. "Margot said that you were, and I quote, *the real thing*. She said you could have told her Fifi was happy and well."

"I wasn't able to establish contact with Fifi, so I had no reason to tell Mrs Chapman anything of the sort."

"And what do you think of your colleagues who *did* tell Margot they were able to contact Fifi?"

Dangerous waters. I thought before I spoke.

"I guess every speaker has their own methods and processes. And it's possible that what works for one person simply doesn't work for another. I can't criticise my colleagues for what the spirits have or haven't told them on a particular day."

"I see. And who do you think is at fault when the psychic supposedly can't *connect* with the spirits?"

"I don't think anyone's at fault. We know so little about how this ability works. Where exactly are these spirits? And how is it that a lucky few of us are able to communicate with them? We're privileged enough to be able to make contact *some* of the time. Do we have any right to complain if we can't make contact every time we want it?"

Lola pouted. It was obviously not the answer she wanted, but the professional smile quickly returned.

"So Ms Marks, I'm sure you realise that for professional reasons, I need to validate your story as much as I can."

My story? She was the one who came to me.

"So I'd like you to contact an old friend for me."

She gave me another of those wide-eyed stares.

"I can try," I said. "Who do you want to speak with?"

"Carla Johansson," she said.

"And how old was Carla when she passed?"

"Nineteen."

Lola's smooth veneer cracked a little. Whoever this friend was, Lola hadn't got over her death yet.

I leaned back in my chair and closed my eyes. I could feel Gray's presence.

"Speak to me, spirits. I seek contact with Carla Johansson, aged nineteen."

I held my breath and hoped this wouldn't be one of the tricky ones, but Gray responded almost immediately.

"She's here, Dorothy. I don't think she's pleased to see Lola, though."

"Lola, Carla is here, but she's not happy about being called. Did you two have a falling out before her death?"

Lola took so long to answer that I opened my eyes to see if she was still there and caught her wiping away a tear.

"We had a fight," she said. "I barely remember what it was about. Something stupid."

"Carla doesn't seem to have forgotten. She says you stole her boyfriend and when she confronted you about it, you laughed."

Lola let out a shaky breath. "We were just teenagers and they weren't all that serious."

"Carla says she was in love with him and that you knew it."

"Puppy love." Lola sniffed. "It wouldn't have lasted, especially when he was happy to go after any girl who showed the slightest bit of interest. I did her a favour. She wouldn't have known what he was really like otherwise."

"I don't think Carla sees it that way," I said. "She sounds like she's still pretty upset. Are you sure you don't have anything you want to say about that while you can?"

She sniffed again. "Carla was like a sister to me and she knows it. If she thought it through, she would see it was for the best."

"Carla's gone, Dorothy," Gray says. "Her parting comment was that she never wants to speak to Lola again."

"I'm afraid she's gone now," I said. "She has asked that you don't call for her again."

Lola wiped one last tear away. How had she managed to cry without her makeup running? I would look like a mess if I did that.

"Well, Dorothy." She resumed her usual composure and gave me a wide-eyed look. "Do you have any closing comments you'd like to make?"

Not really was what I wanted to say, but Lola obviously expected more.

"I'd just like to say that the spirits have given me a great privilege in allowing me to contact them. I don't know why they've chosen me, but I'm very appreciative. We can't underestimate the guidance that those who have passed can give us.

"I see. Well Dorothy, thank you *so* much for your time this morning. It has been *most* enlightening. I'm going to dash back to the office now and hopefully pull this story together before my afternoon deadline."

Another of those expectant pauses.

"Good luck with that," I offered, unsure what else she might be waiting for.

Another pause. When it became obvious that I wasn't going to volunteer any last-minute secrets, Lola packed away her notebook and recorder with a small sigh. She held out her hand and offered me another perfect smile.

"Thanks again, Dorothy. Keep an eye on the next few editions of *The Brisbane Journal* and you should see our story in print very soon."

"I will."

Our story?

She left and I had the distinct impression that she was unhappy with me. Whether it was because I didn't say what she wanted, or because the conversation with her friend hadn't been what she expected, I wasn't sure. It seemed like there was a subtext to my conversation with Lola, a deeper, hidden meaning that I didn't understand. I almost dreaded seeing what would end up in print.

That was my first interview and I didn't exactly enjoy it. I've never been one to go chasing after fame and celebrity, despite what people think. I only ever wanted to help. The way it turned out... Well, that was never what I intended.

My first client for the day wasn't due for an hour, so I decided to take myself for a walk, just to get out of the house for a little while. As long as I was back well ahead of the client's arrival time, Ms Bossypants — AKA Bec — wouldn't give me a hard time. Geez, my life was weird. Who else had to worry about a dead invisible housemate nagging them about being late? I grabbed my mobile and headed for the front door.

"I'll be back soon," I called for the benefit of anyone who might be silently hanging around. Gray wasn't there, but I couldn't always tell when the others were around.

My mobile rang just as I put my hand on the doorknob. I hesitated, but it could be a prospective client. I hit the answer button with a sigh. My tenuous financial circumstances meant I couldn't afford to pass up any opportunity for new clients.

"Hello, this is Dorothy." I set the phone to speaker and tapped the calendar app to check the date of my next available appointment.

"Oh, I'm so glad you answered," a woman said, then burst into tears.

CHAPTER
NINETEEN

I tried not to sigh as the woman started sobbing.

"Margo Chapman said you could help me," the caller said between hiccups. "Can I come and see you?"

I could tell her I was booked out for the next few weeks and by the time her appointment came around, she'd be calmer. If I could get off the phone quickly, I'd still have time for a walk before my first client. As I considered fobbing her off, my conscience prodded me. I got into this gig because I wanted to help people. Well, here was someone who needed my help.

"How far away are you?" I asked.

"Not far." Another hiccup. "Actually, I'm parked in your driveway."

I tried not to let her hear my sigh.

"I only have half an hour, but I could see you now."

No sooner had I hung up than the doorbell rang. Trying not to feel bitter about my lost opportunity to get out of the house, I opened the door.

She was small and fragile. Strands of dark hair hung limply around a face wet with tears. Her eyes were red and swollen from crying. Dark clothes at least a size too big obscured her figure. She looked up at me with an embarrassed half-smile and my resentment dissolved.

"Please, come in." I opened the door wider and stepped aside.

She hesitated, throwing one last look back at her car as if she hadn't quite decided whether to do this. Eventually, she came in. I closed the door and walked over to the chairs, expecting her to follow. She waited by the door, like a wild animal that wasn't sure whether it was safe to come closer.

"Come sit down." I gave her what I hoped was a reassuring smile. "We can talk about what brings you here today."

I saw her deep intake of breath before she shuffled over and sat on the edge of a chair, clutching her handbag with both hands as if to anchor it. Or perhaps to anchor herself.

"I'm Dorothy," I said. "And you are?"

"Simone," she said in a voice that was little more than a whisper. "My name is Simone."

At least she was sure about that.

"How can I help you, Simone?"

Tears rolled down her cheeks. I tried to keep my face blank, not wanting her to see my pity.

"I want to contact my husband, Ben. Ben Whitelock."

"How old was Ben when he passed?"

"Twenty-four."

"And how long has it been since Ben passed?"

My voice was calm and professional. I was getting good at this.

"Eleven days."

My mouth fell open and I closed it. I stared at her in silence, trying to find some words, any words. What do you say to a young woman who has lost her husband less than two weeks ago? I hadn't yet tried to contact a spirit who had died so recently. Was there an initial period when they couldn't be contacted? I was about to find out.

I closed my eyes. Both Gray and Bec had arrived by now. Lissa seemed to be absent, for which I was thankful. I didn't want her to witness this one. As usual, I didn't know whether Samson was here.

"Speak to me, spirits. I'm calling Ben Whitelock, aged twenty-four."

The words were barely out of my mouth before Bec answered.

"He's here, Dorothy. He says to tell his Mone that he loves her."

"I've made contact, Simone. He calls you Mone and says he loves you."

Simone's face crumpled and she covered it with her hands. Her shoulders shook as she sobbed.

Bec relayed Ben's words, speaking so swiftly that I fought to keep up.

"He wants you to remember the time you picnicked in the national park. You went out the day before to buy a picnic basket because you insisted a picnic required a picnic basket. You wrapped a red ribbon around the handle. The lunch you packed was his favourite: egg sandwiches, chocolate biscuits and lemonade. He says you hate egg and chocolate, and yet you ate them without complaint. He never loved you more than that day."

It was a sweet memory and I had difficulty keeping my voice steady. Simone didn't seem to have anything to say or if she did, she was crying too hard. I was almost relieved when Bec said that Ben was leaving.

"I'm about to lose contact with Ben, Simone," I said. "Is there anything you want to say before he goes?"

With a sniff, Simone tried to pull herself together.

"Tell him I love him and I miss him and—" She stopped, eyes wild. "I don't know what else to say. I didn't believe Margot when she said you could contact him. I would have..."

I knew what she wanted to say. That she would have prepared a thoughtful and inspiring message if she had really believed such contact was possible. Instead, she faced the possibility that this was the last time she would speak to him and she was scrounging around for something meaningful to say.

Bec cut in.

"Ben says he knows. That everything she wants to say, he knows."

I relayed the comment and the expression that crossed Simone's face told me the message contained some private meaning known to the two of them.

"Tell him I know too." Tears trickled down her face again. "Tell him I'll always love him."

"He heard that, Dorothy," Bec said. "But he's gone now."

"I'm sorry, Simone," I said. "I've lost contact. But Ben heard your last words."

She gave me a broken smile. "Thank you. You don't know—"

"It's all right," I said. "I know."

She opened her handbag and pulled out a purse. "I didn't even think to ask what you charge. I don't usually have much cash on me. Do you take card?"

"There's no charge today."

I couldn't charge her. This was what I'd got into this business for. Simone shook her head and started to protest, but I leaned across the coffee table to place my hand on her arm.

"Really, Simone, it's fine. If you come back, it's a hundred and fifty dollars an hour. But today is on me."

She swallowed hard and I knew she was fighting tears again. Or still.

"Thank you," was all she said and then she left, letting herself out the front door and closing it gently behind her.

I stayed where I was, too exhausted to move.

"Well done, Dorothy." Bec's words were unusually complimentary.

I nodded, unable to respond.

"You did good, Dorothy," Samson said.

I hadn't even realised he was here. I nodded again. It was beyond me to even open my mouth right now. I sat there for several minutes, not even thinking, until Bec intervened.

"Dorothy, it's almost ten-fifteen according to the kitchen clock and your diary says your client is due at half past. You need to go wash your face and tidy your hair."

I didn't have the energy to get up.

"It'll be fine. I'll just wait here until the client arrives."

"You need to get up," she said. "I know that consultation was intense, but you have to move on. And by the way, I don't think you can afford to do free consultations. You should have charged her."

"I couldn't." I wanted to tell Bec to back off, but that would mean spending the rest of the day placating her. So as tired as I was, I tried to be diplomatic. "She needed me more than anyone else so far. And besides—" I had a moment of inspired genius "—she's going to recommend me to everyone she knows. I'll get so much extra business from her recommendations that I think I can afford to not charge her. It will be worth it."

"Hmm," she said, and I knew I had won this round.

CHAPTER

TWENTY

After my next client left, I sank down into one of the wingback chairs. It had been a long morning. First the interview with Lola, then Simone and her eleven-day-dead husband. Fortunately, the next consultation had been easier, but they were all emotional and I was wrung out.

"You need to get moving if you want to eat before the next one." Bec's voice was irritated and I had no doubt that she deliberately let me hear it. She seemed to take it as a personal insult when I needed to rest.

"I'm not hungry." I didn't move from where I sat, slumped in my chair with my eyes closed and my head resting on the back. "Maybe you could wake me up just before the next one's due?"

Something poked me in the stomach and I jerked awake. Of course, I was the only visible person in the room. I should also be the only person here with the ability to impact on the physical plane.

"Time to get up." Bec's voice sounded strained, just as it always did before she got majorly upset with me.

"Bec, I'm exhausted—"

Another sharp jab in the stomach.

"Ow. What was that?"

"I'm warning you." Surprise edged her voice.

"Bec, I don't—" The chair tipped right up and tossed me onto the floor.

"Hey, how did you do that?" I was more startled than angry as I picked myself up.

"I warned you."

"So now you can poke me and tip over my chair?" I didn't need Bec thinking she could run my life. I appreciated her help in keeping my appointments straight, but she had to remember who the living person was around here. "Since when can you do stuff like that?"

"Since now, I guess." She sounded unsure.

"How did you do that, Bec?" Gray's voice was calm, but he must be dying to know her secret.

"I don't know," she said. "I just imagined myself poking her in the stomach."

"I'm so glad I give you plenty to think about," I said.

They ignored me.

"And then what?" he asked.

"I don't know. It just sort of happened."

"How did you tip over the chair?"

"I wanted Dorothy to get up, so I imagined the chair tipping her out and then it did."

I rightened my chair as they spoke and, without thinking, flopped back into it. That apparently didn't go unnoticed.

"Do you think you could do it again?" Gray asked.

A brief respite. Then I was face-down on the carpet, the chair on top of me.

"Oh, come on." I pushed the chair off and hauled myself to

my feet. "Give me a break, guys. I just want to sit for a bit. I'm exhausted."

Neither of them bothered to respond. I sat the chair upright again.

"You try, Gray," Bec said.

There was a pause.

"Go on," she said.

"I'm trying," he said with a grunt. "Nothing's happening."

"You just have to picture the chair tipping over."

"It's not working."

"Maybe Dorothy needs to be in it," Bec said. "Dorothy—"

"Don't even think about it." I inspected the carpet burn on my palms. "I will not sit there just so you have the fun of tipping me out. What are you, five years old?"

"This is very exciting, Dorothy," Bec said. "We've never been able to move things in your world before."

"Thank goodness," I said.

"I don't think you have any concept of what this means for us," she snapped.

I swallowed a sharp retort. It had to be hard for them, just hanging around and watching me all day. Nobody to talk to except each other and me and the spirits my clients asked for.

"I'm sorry, Bec. That wasn't how I meant it. I realise this is a big deal for you, but it's painful getting thrown out like that. And I don't want to be tiptoeing around my own home, too scared to sit down in case someone decides to see if they can throw me off the furniture. So you've got to promise you won't do it again, okay?"

She was silent.

"Bec? I'm serious. We need ground rules here. I don't mind you guys trying to move other stuff, but I want to know that when I sit on something, it's not going to throw me off."

"We agree, Dorothy." Gray's voice was as implacable as ever. "I apologise. We got a bit excited. This is not something we ever expected to be able to do. Perhaps these abilities develop the longer we're here."

"I get it, Gray, I do. But I want to hear Bec say she agrees, too."

Silence. Great. That meant Bec was in a mood again.

"Bec? I mean it. I want your agreement that you will not try to tip over any item of furniture I'm sitting on."

"Fine," she said eventually.

"Fine, what?"

"I agree."

Her tone said otherwise, but I ignored it. Perhaps now I could sit and rest for a few minutes before my next client. My butt had barely touched the chair before I felt Bec bristle. I tensed, waiting for the chair to throw me out again.

"What are you doing?" Bec's voice held an edge of warning.

"I'm going to rest for a bit. I thought—"

"You thought wrong. You look a mess. Go have a shower and you should eat something. You have a full afternoon and you can't do that on an empty stomach."

Her tone told me there was no point arguing. I headed for the bathroom.

"Less than sixty minutes until the appointment," Bec called after me. "And I want you ready a full thirty minutes before she's due."

"Yes, mother," I muttered.

To give Bec credit, I felt refreshed after a shower. As my exhaustion flowed away down the drain, my stomach grumbled. Bec was right. I couldn't possibly get through the afternoon without some food.

As soon as I was dressed, I went to the kitchen and made a humongous ham and salad sandwich. I gulped it down and could have made a good dent in a second one, except that by then Bec was moaning about how my client was due in exactly thirty minutes and I wasn't ready. I threw my dishes in the sink, ducked upstairs to brush my teeth, and was waiting in the lounge room with twenty-five minutes to spare.

CHAPTER

TWENTY-ONE

I woke unusually early on Monday morning, having slept somewhat restlessly thanks to a bottle of wine with dinner. After a coffee and some breakfast, I walked down to the newsagent to pick up a copy of *The Brisbane Journal*. I'll admit I was excited about the prospect of my interview appearing in print, and more than a little apprehensive about how I would come across.

I went straight home with the paper and didn't let myself look inside until I was seated at the kitchen counter with another coffee. Heart pounding, I read the lead article on the front page, determined not to flick through and look for Lola's story. That resolution lasted only until Lissa arrived.

"Well?" she said.

"Well, what?"

"Is your interview in there? What does it say?"

And there went my resolve. I flicked through the next few pages. The headline on page six jumped out at me: *Local psychic the "real deal"*.

"Oh geez."

The phone rang before I could read any further. It was a new client and I made an appointment with her for six weeks' time. She was quite pushy about not being able to wait that long and I had to tell her several times that I couldn't do anything earlier. She mentioned she had seen the story about me in *The Brisbane Journal*.

The red voicemail light was on by the time I hung up, but the phone rang again before I could check my messages. Another new client. Then a local radio station, a newspaper — one that was delivered country-wide — and another new client. I hung up, eyeing the clock. I had to switch the phone to voicemail right now or risk being stuck here when my first client arrived. The phone rang again.

"Dorothy, this is Mary Simons," the caller said. "I'm an executive assistant with Channel OneTV. I'm ringing to see whether you would be interested in being interviewed on *The City Tonight*, OneTV's evening current affairs program."

Holy crap.

"Jena Mitchell, one of our star reporters, would be the one to interview you. She's extremely interested to speak with you."

I made myself wait before responding. Of course I would say yes, but I didn't want to sound too keen.

"Jena has had a long-time fascination with the paranormal," Mary rushed on. "So, of course she'll be very sympathetic to your story."

She stopped talking and I made myself count to five. Just as I opened my mouth to respond, she upped the ante.

"And of course, we'd be willing to pay you for the interview."

"Really?" It was out of my mouth before I could stop myself. Although I had a steady stream of clients at the moment, who knew how long that would last? The spirits might tire of helping me or my ability to hear them might disappear as suddenly as it had appeared. I needed to jump on any other opportunity to make some money.

"Five thousand dollars," she said.

My jaw dropped. When I didn't respond, she must have misinterpreted my disbelief at such an exorbitant amount for disinterest.

"Of course, we realise your story is hot-hot-hot at the moment." She spoke quickly now and sounded nervous. "Perhaps we could increase that to seven and a half."

"Seven and a half?"

"I'm sorry, seven and a half thousand is the most I'm authorised to offer. If that isn't acceptable, I'd have to speak to my executive producer and see whether he's willing to offer more."

How far could I push my luck?

"Perhaps you should do that." I tried to sound nonchalant, although I wasn't sure I pulled it off. "I'm very busy. In fact, I'm booked out for weeks ahead at the moment. It would have to be an amount that would be worth my while to squeeze you in."

"Absolutely." She still sounded worried. "I completely understand. Just so I can make sure I'm asking for approval for a high enough offer, what amount would you be looking for?"

Geez, what should I say? I've never been one to read those trashy women's magazines that report how much various celebrities got paid for interviews.

"Twenty thousand," I said. "And then I'll consider it."

Of course, if she came back with an offer of ten thousand, I'd say yes immediately. I would have taken five if she hadn't offered more so quickly.

"Right. Twenty thousand. Let me see what I can do. Can I call you back in about an hour?"

I glanced at the time. Bec would be on my case pretty soon.

"I'll be with a client, but you can leave a message on my voicemail and if the offer's acceptable, I'll get back to you."

"Great, that's a plan. I'll talk to you soon."

The phone rang again the moment I hung up. I answered, not quite suppressing a sigh. My reluctance quickly turned to amazement as I discovered the caller this time was from a rival channel's current affairs program. I hesitantly told him I was already negotiating with OneTV.

"And how much have they offered you?" he asked. His voice was smooth and he didn't sound fazed in the slightest.

"We haven't settled on an amount yet." I felt like a traitor to OneTV. After all, they got in first.

"We'll double whatever they offer," he said.

I was glad he couldn't see me. I seemed to be spending a lot of time today with my mouth hanging open.

"I'll give you my direct number. Call me as soon as you have a final offer from OneTV and we'll double it."

"Do you have to get authorisation for that?" I asked, feeling quite the pro.

"Sweetie, I am the authorisation," he said. "Channel Three doesn't send lowly assistants to make offers like some other channels do."

"Oh." Now I just felt like an idiot.

"Do you have a pen? Here's my number. And I want you to call me the minute you get off the phone from OneTV. Okay?"

"Okay," I said faintly and jotted his number down.

I switched the phone to voicemail as soon as I hung up and took a moment to stare down at the phone number in my diary. I circled it and wrote "Channel Three" and "x2" next to it. As if I would forget whose number it was.

I glanced at the clock. Forty minutes until the client was due. Bec would be almost ready to start nagging. But wow. Two

TV channels fighting it out to interview me. Even if one of them didn't know yet that they were fighting. I felt Bec arrive.

"I'm moving," I said before she could speak. "I know I've got forty minutes."

"Thirty-eight actually."

"I'm just going to have a quick shower."

My first client that morning, Mrs Liu, arrived exactly on time. The day was uneventful except that after my last client it took me three hours to call everyone who had left voicemail messages.

Mary Simons from OneTV had called to say her executive producer had authorised payment of twenty thousand dollars. I listened to her message twice to be sure I hadn't misheard it and slowly wrote the amount in my diary.

Twenty thousand dollars.

That was more than I would normally earn in six months, by the time I paid tax. And I could make that in, what, an hour? Two hours maybe? I supposed that for a TV interview I'd have to spend time in hair and makeup, but even allowing for that, twenty thousand dollars was a huge amount. And Channel Three would double it. In a couple of hours I could make more than usually went into my bank account in a year. It was difficult to comprehend, but it would certainly ease my financial woes, for a while at least.

I dialled the number for the executive producer from Channel Three. It was only a little after five and I hoped it wasn't too late to call.

"Jeremy Jacobs," he answered crisply on the second ring.

"This is Dorothy Marks," I said. "I spoke to you this morning—"

"Oh yes, Dorothy, how are you, sweetheart? Did you hear from OneTV?"

"Yes, I did. That's why I'm calling."

"And how much have they offered?"

I took a deep breath.

"Twenty thousand dollars."

"Fine, we'll double it," he said without a moment's hesitation. "When are you available? We want to strike while the iron's hot, so to speak. Could we come to your place tomorrow?"

I didn't know what to say. I hadn't expected him to agree, let alone so quickly.

"Um, I'm just checking my diary," I said, more to give myself a moment to think than anything else.

A funny feeling in the pit of my stomach told me this would be one of those moments that changed everything. But what was I giving up? I was unemployed and every one of my friends was somebody else's dearly departed. Forty thousand was a lot of money and if I was sensible, between that and my clients, I could make it last two years or even more. Two years before I had to look for another job. And in the meantime, I could really help people. My life might change irrevocably, but I knew I was making the right decision.

"My last client should be gone by four-thirty," I said. "Would five p.m. be too late?"

"I'd like your story to make our evening show tomorrow," he said. "Do you have any time in the morning?"

"I'm sorry." I checked my diary again. "My first client's due at nine-thirty and—"

"We could come over before that," he said. "Would six-thirty suit you? We could be filming by about seven-fifteen and we'll make sure we're done by nine-fifteen."

Forty thousand dollars.

"Okay. But we'll need to be finished by nine. My clients are often early. Will that be a problem?"

He hummed for a moment as if mentally running through a schedule. "Let's make it six a.m."

He hung up and I stood there, staring at the phone in my hand. Forty thousand dollars for less than three hours of work. Was that even legal?

As for Lola's newspaper article, I never got around to reading past the heading. By the time I next thought about it, more than a year later, it didn't matter anymore what Lola James had said about me.

CHAPTER

TWENTY-TWO

I was up at five the next morning, figuring that if I didn't eat early, I might not get a chance until lunch. Truth be told, I had been lying awake for hours, too busy freaking out to sleep. I forced myself to eat a single slice of toast. By five-thirty, I waited in the lounge room. The spirits gathered around me. They were unusually silent, but their presence steadied my nerves a little. At five-fifty, the doorbell rang and two women swept in.

"Hi there, Dorothy," one of them said with a breezy smile as she laid two small suitcases on my coffee table. "We're here to do your hair and makeup. You just sit right here for me."

They kept me occupied with small talk while they worked. At six-thirty, the door opened and the journalist swanned in. I recognised her immediately. Maree Onassis. Small, dark-haired and brash. The type who would knock on someone's door, then when they tried to slam it shut, stick a foot inside to jam the door open. I started to wonder whether I had made a big mistake until she handed me an envelope.

"Your cheque, Dorothy," Maree said with a smile that was nothing but sweet.

"Thank you."

I stared down at the envelope, wondering whether it would be bad form to open it.

"It's okay if you want to check it." She was obviously accustomed to this response. "You won't offend me."

I couldn't open it after that.

"Thanks, but it's not necessary."

I tucked the envelope into my pocket. Forty thousand dollars. I just had to get through the next couple of hours.

Later, I didn't have much memory of Maree's interview, other than how nervous I was. They had to stop the cameras twice to let me calm down. I didn't see the interview when it aired that evening as I was too busy returning phone calls, but I've been told I appeared confident and sincere. And if I thought my phone had gone nuts after *The Brisbane Journal* interview, that was nothing compared to the reaction to my first television interview.

Over the next few days, media outlets from all over the country bombarded me with requests for interviews. Print and radio journalists flew in to interview me. Television channels from three states sent filming crews. Two women's magazines battled it out for an exclusive photo shoot. The offers came in so quickly I could hardly keep track of them and I was beyond exhausted from squeezing in interviews before and after my clients and throughout the weekend. Within two weeks, I had cheques totalling almost two hundred thousand dollars, although I had yet to find time to take them to the bank.

I sat up late every night returning calls, emails and even snail mail. The number of letters I received through the post surprised me. In these days of email and text, I rarely received anything in the mail other than bills. Now I received letter after letter from strangers, although I didn't know how they had found my address. Some asked whether I planned to tour and if so, could I please come to their city. Others begged for free consultations and included lengthy details of their financial circumstances. I painstakingly replied to every message.

This is a business, Bec had said when I raised the possibility of accepting some of those requests for free consultations. Would you expect your hairdresser to cut your hair for free because you couldn't afford to pay?

I conceded she had a point, although I wasn't sure I agreed. Why should my ability be limited to those who had the means to pay?

It was well after midnight on a Tuesday as I sat in the kitchen, the counter buried under piles of letters, notes and to-do lists. My diary lay open on top of a stack of cheques. I really needed to go to the bank. Maybe I could do it on Saturday morning.

"You can't go on like this," Gray said.

I had been too busy mopping up some spilled wine to notice his arrival. It was a shame that Bec's burgeoning ability to impact on the physical world didn't extend to helping with the cleaning. She hadn't tipped me off any more furniture. Maybe she couldn't even do it anymore. I didn't want to ask in case she got angry with me.

"He's right," Bec said. "You need an assistant."

I laughed as I tossed the wine-soaked cloth in the sink.

"An assistant? What on earth for?"

"Look at you," Bec said. "You're up late every night returning calls, making appointments, trying to keep your finances straight. You don't have time for these things. Sooner or later, it's going to affect your work because you'll be too tired to concentrate."

"I can't afford an assistant."

"Are you kidding?" She snorted. "Have you looked at those cheques? From what I've seen, you have enough to live on and still pay wages for a part-time assistant for five years. You could hire someone on a temporary basis, maybe six months. A couple of hours a day. That would free you up so that you could spend some time recharging in the evenings. Get some exercise. Cook a decent meal for a change instead of microwaving that frozen junk. Maybe you could even do some housework and, lord knows, the house needs it."

"I know I'm a bit behind on the housework."

There had been no time to do anything more than rinse out a coffee cup and give the benches the briefest of wipes. Breakfast had become toast buttered on the bench and eaten over the sink to avoid washing a plate. Lunch and dinner were frozen junk, as Bec put it. They weren't that bad. Not tasty, but food was food and most evenings I was so exhausted I didn't much care what I ate as long as I could prepare it with minimal effort.

"A bit behind?" Bec said. "Dorothy, the only room you've vacuumed in the last four weeks is the lounge. It's also the only room that's received even the most cursory of dusting. I happen to know the oven contains an assortment of dishes you never got around to washing. I don't know when you last changed your bed sheets and the laundry is going to take a week to work through. You've got to get some help around here."

"I don't have time to find someone." I knew I sounded whiney, but I already felt overwhelmed and Bec was making it worse. "Yes, an assistant would be brilliant, especially if she could give me a hand with the housework, but it takes time to hire someone. You need to write an advertisement, put it up online, wait for people to apply, read applications..."

"Or you can use a recruitment agency." Bec's tone said how stupid she thought I was. "You ring and tell them what you want. They interview the applicants and pick someone. You pay over the phone and wait for your new assistant to arrive."

"Really? They do everything?"

"You need this, Dorothy, and what's more, you can afford it. Even if you didn't take another client for the rest of the year, you could still afford it."

"Not that there'd be much point in hiring an assistant if I wasn't taking any more clients," I muttered.

Bec heard me. I knew she would.

"That's hardly the point." The chill in her voice told me I would regret my hasty comment. "The point is that you're drowning and you need an assistant."

I poured the last of the wine into my glass. "Okay, I'll ring a recruitment agency in the morning."

"Your first client is due at nine-thirty as usual, but you should be able to find an agency that's open before then. You can at least put the wheels in motion."

"Yes, Bec." I went back to the letter I was trying to write a response to. "It's a pity you couldn't be my assistant. You're good at keeping me organised."

"Unfortunately, I can't answer the phone or write appointments in your diary or bank the cheques or any of those other useful things a living assistant could do."

She sounded even frostier now. It was a thoughtless thing to say. I drained my wine with a sigh. Making up with Bec required a level of sobriety that I didn't have right now.

"Sorry, Bec. It was meant to be a compliment."

"Some compliment," she said with a sniff. "Go to bed. The rest of that can wait until tomorrow. You're too drunk to do anything properly, anyway."

I opened my mouth to argue but realised she was right. My head was far too fuzzy to think clearly about anything simple, let alone come up with a coherent response to the woman who insisted she desperately needed to contact her dearly departed great grandmother, but couldn't afford to pay for my services because she was a single mother of seven children, surviving on a disability pension with irregular and minuscule cheques from her no-good-dirt-bag-of-an-ex-husband. She would have to wait until I was sober.

TWENTY-THREE

Saturday finally arrived and I couldn't have been more ready for the weekend. I had messages to return as well as cash and cheques to bank. Had it only been a month since Mrs Chapman's consultation? If I continued to be this busy, I wasn't in any danger of defaulting on my mortgage. Unless, of course, I didn't go to the bank.

I did that as soon as it opened, then spent the rest of the morning returning calls. I booked out another couple of weeks' worth of appointments. It was a good feeling to see all those appointments in my diary. Some would likely cancel or just not turn up, but I had so many lined up that even if a third didn't happen, it wouldn't be a problem.

There had been no other calls about the secretarial services I had intended to offer. I should take down those signs the next time I went to the supermarket. I would feel terrible if someone rang about getting something typed up and I had to turn them away, but I didn't have time for that now.

I didn't realise it was well after noon until my stomach growled. Actually, it had been growling for a while, but I had been ignoring it with the thought of "just one more phone call".

I should stop and at least make myself a sandwich, if I even had any food. I needed to get to the supermarket today and I could take down those signs at the same time.

I found enough in the fridge for a salad sandwich. There was bread that was only a little stale, lettuce, a cucumber that didn't look too shrivelled, half a tomato, and some cheese. Not a terribly substantial lunch, but it would do.

I tossed the salad ingredients on the counter and went back to the fridge for the butter. As I put my sandwich together, I couldn't find the cucumber. Figuring I had left it in the fridge, I rummaged through the vegetable crisper, but it didn't seem to be there. I turned back to the counter and there was the cucumber sitting right beside my half-made sandwich. I was too tired to even make a simple sandwich. Maybe I should take a break from answering messages this afternoon and spend some time relaxing.

I sliced the cucumber and reached for the tomato. It wasn't there. I was certain it had been sitting right beside the cucumber a moment ago, but now it was under the lettuce. Then when I went to pick up the cheese, that too wasn't where I had thought.

"You're losing your mind, Dorothy," I said to myself as I checked the fridge for the third time. Sure enough, when I turned back to the counter, the cheese was sitting right where I had expected it to be.

It wasn't until Lissa giggled that I realised what was happening.

"Dorothy, I can move things now," she said.

Her voice was as light as ever, but her words left me feeling a little chilled. First Bec and now Lissa.

"How excellent for you," I said. "How did you figure it out?"

"I don't know. After Bec realised she could push you out of the chair, I just started experimenting."

"Well, maybe you could stop moving the things I'm trying to make my sandwich with."

I reached for the knife, but it slid right out of my grasp and skidded along the kitchen counter. My heart pounded a little harder and it was only when my chest began to ache that I realised I had forgotten to breathe.

"Was that you too, Lissa?"

A giggle was her only reply.

Tipping me out of chairs and hiding salad ingredients was one thing, but being able to move a knife, that made me feel very uncomfortable. If Lissa could push the knife along the counter, what else could she do with it? What else might she do while she was experimenting, as she put it, perhaps without realising the consequences? Could she lift the knife through the air? Could she cut me with it?

"You should see your face, Dorothy."

Lissa's voice was merry and the knife slid back along the counter towards me. I slapped my hand over it to stop it.

"Stop that, Lissa. It isn't funny."

For the first time, I started to wonder whether I could really trust my new spirit friends.

TWENTY-FOUR

My new assistant, Em Reed, started the following Monday. Calm and efficient, she had jet black hair cut in a sleek bob, olive skin and a Latino look to her face. The recruitment agency had arranged for her to work four hours a day on a trial basis for a month, with two hours to be devoted to organising my life and two hours towards creating some sort of order in my house.

She already knew that I ran a home-based consulting company. I told her what times I usually scheduled my appointments and how much I charged. That seemed to be enough information for Em, as she didn't ask about the exact nature of my business. As I showed her around the house, Em took one look at the kitchen and shook her head.

"I'll start in here," she said.

She had a very no nonsense attitude, much like Bec, and she struck me as the sort of person you didn't argue with.

"Whatever you think," I said and retreated to the lounge room with my diary.

"I'll need that once I'm done in here," she called after me.

"What?"

"The book." She gestured with one arm; the other already held a load of dishes she had collected as she walked through the house. "If I'm going to look after your business affairs, I'll need your appointment book."

"Oh, okay." I looked down at the book in my hands. "Just tell me when you need it."

As I sat in the lounge room, waiting for my first client, I could hear dishes landing in the sink with a splash. A broom knocked at the corners of the room. A thud as Em flung something in the rubbish bin. Several thuds. Maybe she was cleaning out the fridge. I had been meaning to do that.

My business affairs, she had said. I hadn't thought of it in those terms before. It still seemed wrong that I could make so much money so easily. No wonder there were so many fakes out there. I had a never-ending stream of clients and the constant requests for interviews showed no sign of letting up. The newspapers and radio stations rarely paid, but the TV channels and magazines did and those interviews were even more profitable than my clients. The doorbell jarred me from my thoughts.

"I'll get it." Em was by the door before I could even stand up. "What's the client's name?"

I blinked at her in surprise and checked my diary.

"Mrs Rightman."

Em opened the door.

"Mrs Rightman?" She sounded solicitous and welcoming, every inch the professional. "Please come in. Dorothy is expecting you. I hope you are well today?"

She kept up a steady stream of small talk as she seated Mrs Rightman in front of me.

"Coffee? A glass of water, perhaps?"

"Water would be good," Mrs Rightman whispered. "Only if it's not too much trouble."

"No trouble at all," Em assured her and bustled off.

Mrs Rightman and I looked at each other. I suspected I looked as dazed as she did.

"My new assistant," I said.

"Oh. She seems very good."

Em returned and set a glass of water in front of Mrs Rightman. She had even found a coaster. She placed a glass in front of me as well, then disappeared back into the kitchen. I was a little worried that her thumping and banging would be too loud during my session, but never heard a sound out of Em until she swept back in to collect the payment and usher Mrs Rightman out.

Em closed the door and turned back to me.

"Right then, I need your appointment book."

I handed it over.

"You said the next client would be due at eleven?" She flipped through pages of my almost-illegible scrawl and frowned. She had obviously already decided she had to do something about my diary.

"Yes."

"Right, back to the kitchen, then. There's a small snack for you on the counter. You should take a few minutes to rest while I tidy up out here."

What could I say in the face of such efficiency? I retreated to the kitchen while she breezed around the front room, removing the glasses and doing I don't know what else. The effect was obvious, though. When I returned, the room looked fresher and straighter.

"Fifteen minutes until the next one, Dorothy," she said as she swept back to the kitchen. "A Ms Hathson."

CHAPTER

TWENTY-FIVE

leven a.m. came and went with no sign of my second client. By half past, I was ready to write her off, but at last the doorbell rang. Em ushered in a frazzled woman who looked like she was around thirty years old.

"I'm sorry I'm late." Her voice trembled. "I, um, had trouble finding you."

"Really?"

I lived on a major street and the house number was displayed in large letters on the fence. She looked away and didn't answer. We sat on the wingback chairs. My previous clients had seated themselves and then looked at me expectantly, waiting for the show. Ms Hathson — she had been very particular about the Ms — simply looked away. She rubbed her thumbnail against the side of her forefinger and didn't show any curiosity about our session. I forced a smile that I hoped was both welcoming and inviting.

"Ms Hathson, who would you like me to contact for you?"

She looked down at her hands, still rubbing that thumbnail against her finger. Then at her shoes. Then around the room. Finally, she looked back at me.

"My husband." She sounded as if she had only just decided.

"And what is his name?"

"It *was* Michael Bright." Quite a lot of emphasis on the *was*.

"His age?"

"Thirty-one."

"How long has it been since he passed?"

"Three years."

Ms Hathson had been widowed young. How long would it take to recover from her loss and move on with her life? Perhaps that was what today's visit was about. Maybe she had met someone else and wanted her husband's blessing before she proceeded.

I closed my eyes.

"Speak to me, spirits. I'm looking for Michael Bright, aged thirty-one."

Gray's response was immediate, although his voice was strained.

"Hold on, Dorothy."

I waited. After a minute or two, I opened my eyes and smiled at Ms Hathson.

"My spirit contacts are just trying to connect with your husband. Sometimes it takes a little while."

It didn't, but I felt like I had to explain the delay somehow. Ms Hathson nodded, looking almost surprised, and returned to her perusal of her shoes.

"Dorothy, we have the husband here."

Gray sounded odd, but I ignored the feeling of reluctance that gave me.

"Good news, Ms Hathson," I said brightly. "I've made contact with Michael."

"And how is the lying bastard?" she asked.

I didn't have to wait long for Gray's response.

"Her husband says — and I'm giving you the edited

version here — that he hopes his bitchy slut of a wife has managed to make something of her life, although he doubts it."

Geez, if that was the edited text, I didn't want the full version. I cleared my throat.

"Ms Hathson, your husband says he hopes you have made something of your life."

It sounded awful, but not nearly as bad as what Gray had said.

"Oh, I bet he did." She smirked. "Were there a few adjectives in there that you didn't pass on?"

I felt a surge of dislike for her, but strove to keep my voice pleasant.

"I don't know what you mean."

"Then it's obviously not Michael you're speaking to, *clairvoyant*." Heavy sarcasm on the last word. "He would never have said something so bland about me."

My patience, which had already frayed at her smirk, snapped.

"I'm not sure what he actually said because my spirit contact tells me he cleaned it up, but the version I got was that Michael hoped his bitchy slut of a wife has made something of her life but he doubted it."

Ms Hathson barked a brief laugh.

"That sounds more like it. Tell the bastard I hope he rots in hell and ask him whether it's hot where he is."

I silently cursed myself for letting my temper get the better of me. I should have pretended I didn't know what she was talking about or I could have even claimed to have unexpectedly lost contact with her husband. Then I could have sent her on her way.

"Dorothy, I can't even tell you what he said to that," Gray said. "Can you do something?"

I tried for a change of topic, hoping it would defuse the situation.

"Ms Hathson, how did your husband die?"

"I murdered the cheating bastard."

Shit shit shit.

"He confirms that," Gray said. "She stabbed him in the heart with a kitchen knife."

I clasped my hands in my lap so she wouldn't see them shaking.

"Ms Hathson, he says you stabbed him in the heart."

She smirked. "It was no more than the lying bastard deserved. Has he told you what he did?"

I shook my head, not trusting my voice. I didn't want to know, but I was pretty sure she was going to tell me.

"I caught him in bed with my little sister. And that wasn't the first time he had cheated on me. He did it over and over. And like a pathetic fool, I kept believing him when he said he would change, that he would stop cheating. That he LOVED ME."

She shouted now.

"And the day I found him with my sister, she was begging him to stop. She said that she'd changed her mind and she didn't want to do it anymore. And what did he do?"

Ms Hathson glared at me, as if daring me to guess. Unable to think of a single thing to say, I shook my head again. I hoped my face didn't reveal my feelings.

"He didn't stop, did he? My cheating bastard of a husband raped my little sister. I saw her naked body after I hauled him off her. Her bruised and bleeding body. She begged him to stop, but the bastard wouldn't."

Gray interrupted her monologue. "He says it was her fault, that he did it to stop her from whining at him. She was always telling him to get his own life, so he did."

I swallowed hard and closed my eyes. Maybe I should write a code of conduct. Something the clients could sign before we started giving me the right to end their consultation at any time without explanation.

"So what does he say to that?" she asked.

Her face was so smug that I wanted to lean across the coffee table and slap the smile right off it. Against my better judgement, I relayed Gray's words.

"It was to stop your whining. It was his way of getting his own life."

She snarled, and I was certain that if her husband was physically present in the room right then, she would have killed him all over again.

"You bastard. You got your own life by raping my little sister? I'm glad I killed you, you sick son of a bitch. I hope you died in agony. I watched your blood soak into the mattress, do you know that? Did you hang around to watch? I pushed your body off the bed and lay in your blood. I slept there that night. Did you see me sleep in your blood with your corpse beside me on the floor?"

My stomach heaved. I could picture the scene so clearly. Her waking up with dried blood flaking off her skin. His body cooling on the floor, rigor mortis setting in. And the sister. Where was she during all this?

"Do you know Peggy killed herself, Michael?"

Oh god. Could it get any worse?

"She couldn't live with what you did, so she washed four packets of painkillers down with a bottle of gin. Do you know who found her? Our mother. Do you have any idea what it does to a woman to find her own daughter dead? Mum's never recovered. She tried to kill herself a few months ago."

Oh shit, going from bad to worse. Worse to worser.

"She slit her wrists. Luckily I found her in time. If she had died, it would be all your fault. Her death would be on your head too."

She paused for breath and Gray took his chance.

"Dorothy, I'm not even going to relay most of what this guy is saying. But the gist of it is that his wife was a frigid bitch, so he raped her sister. He says he can't believe the way she played the cops and got off scot free, but to tell her he's watching everything she does. He wants her to know that he sees it all."

I wanted nothing more than to get this murderous bitch out of my house. I didn't care if I didn't get paid. I just wanted her out of here.

"I think we should finish the consultation, Ms Hathson," I said.

"Dorothy," Gray said. "He's getting pretty agitated you're not passing that on."

No way was I doing that. I shook my head. Ms Hathson would think I was odd, but hopefully Gray would understand.

Then the light bulb blew with spectacular force. I looked up in time to see a shower of sparks arcing out from the bulb. Shattered glass rained down on me.

"Dorothy, I'd suggest you relay his message," Gray said. "Right now."

"That wasn't him, was it?" I was regrettably incautious with my words.

"Did Michael do that?" Ms Hathson asked. "Are you telling me he can do things?"

"Tell her now, Dorothy," Gray said. "Before it's too late."

"I can't."

The front window shattered.

"God damn it, Dorothy," Gray shouted. "Tell her now."

I couldn't even remember what he had said anymore.

"He says you're a frigid bitch."

Ms Hathson snorted. "I expected better than that."

"And he's watching you. Every little thing you do, he's watching you."

For the first time, Ms Hathson looked perturbed.

"Everywhere you go, everything you do, everyone you speak to, he's watching. Waiting."

Okay, so I embellished. It wasn't like she didn't deserve it.

Perturbation gave way to concern. Her face paled a little and she clutched her handbag tighter.

Gray gave me an explicit account of what Michael would do to his young bride if he ever got his hands on her. As I finished relaying this, the front door blew open and slammed against the wall.

Ms Hathson got up and ran.

TWENTY-SIX

The kitchen door opened and Em poked her head out.

"Everything okay out here, Dorothy?"

Her gaze went straight to the broken window and the shattered lightbulb that had rained down on the carpet.

"I'll get the vacuum cleaner," she said.

"Hall closet," I said, a little faintly, as I wondered how to explain what had happened, but Em didn't ask.

"I know. I've already found it."

"He's gone." Gray sounded exhausted rather than relieved. "He followed her."

"That was scary," Lissa said.

I had been so distracted that I hadn't realised she was there.

"How much did you hear, Lissa?" I held my hand over my heart as I waited for it to slow back down to a normal speed.

"Only a little," she said.

"I don't think Lissa should be present for the consultations," Bec said. "That won't be the last one that's too adult for her."

"That's not fair," Lissa said. "It's not like I'm ever going to get any older."

"She has a point, Bec," Gray said.

I cut in before Bec could answer.

"I agree with Gray. I don't think we can or should censor what Lissa hears. We'll just have to help her deal with it. She'll get used to it. We all will."

Em returned with the vacuum cleaner. She looked around the room, as if expecting there to be someone with me. She shook her head a little and shooed me out. Perhaps she had overheard my side of the conversation and wondered who I was talking to. I supposed she would figure out the nature of my consultations soon enough.

I went to the bathroom and tried to get all the shattered light bulb out of my hair. My clothes were speckled with splinters of glass and would need to be thrown out. The spirits had followed me, although they stayed in the bedroom in accordance with the "no spirits in the bathroom" rule. As I went out to the bedroom to grab a change of clothes, Bec was huffing. It seemed the argument between her and Gray had continued.

"Why do I feel like you're all ganging up on me?" she asked.

"We're not ganging up on you," Gray said. "But we can't shelter Lissa from the real world."

"Have you forgotten we're dead?" Bec asked. "It doesn't get much more real than this."

"Bec, sometimes you can be a—"

"Stop fighting." Lissa spoke over the top of Gray. "Just stop it. I hate it when you do this."

"Lissa, love," Bec said.

"Leave me alone," Lissa said. "I don't want to talk to any of you right now."

Her presence seemed to disappear.

"I'll go after her," Samson said. I hadn't even known he was there. "Give her a minute, and I'll go talk to her."

It was the longest sentence I had ever heard from him. I hadn't realised he and Lissa were so close.

"Go on then," Bec said with a sniff. "You're the only one who can ever calm her down when she's in a mood, anyway. Sometimes I just don't know what to do with that girl."

"She'll be fine," Gray said. "Samson will calm her down and she'll be back soon, meek as pie and feeling a bit embarrassed about having a tantrum in front of Dorothy."

That pulled me up short. Here I was, thinking of us as a family of sorts, squabbling and then making peace, but they viewed me as an outsider. I knew nothing about their lives on the other side of the veil and had never even wondered what they did when they weren't with me. I was ashamed of my self-ishness, but this wasn't the right time for questions. I finally realised they were still waiting for my response to Gray's statement.

"It didn't bother me," I said. "Perhaps we've been forgetting that she's a teenager."

I sensed Bec's objection and hurried on before she could speak.

"Lissa is fifteen," I said. "She's neither a child nor an adult. She's too old to baby and she's old enough to know it. Also, that spirit was really frightening. You don't have to be fifteen to be scared by him."

"Dorothy's right, Bec," Gray said. "I know Lissa looks like a child, but she's more adult than you give her credit for."

"I'll go apologise," Bec said stiffly.

"Give her some time," Gray said. "Let Samson talk to her first. She'll come back when she's calmed down and you can apologise then."

Bec didn't respond and they were both silent for a while after that. Maybe they blocked me out of a private conversation.

"Have you ever encountered a spirit like that before?" I

hoped they wouldn't realise I only asked to ease my awkwardness about wondering whether they were talking privately.

"No, this was new for all of us," Gray said. "He arrived with her and I could tell straight away that he was furious. I didn't expect him to react the way he did, though. I'm sorry I didn't try to warn you earlier."

"He did some damage in my lounge room."

I searched for a way to ask what I really wanted to know. Bec hadn't tried to tip me out of any more chairs and Lissa had stopped messing with knives. If either Gray or Samson had developed similar abilities, they hadn't mentioned it. I was still trying to find a way to ask about it when Em called up the stairs to me.

"It's almost twelve-fifteen, Dorothy. You might want to come down and have lunch. Next client's due at one."

I inhaled a little shakily. After that last one, I wasn't sure I wanted any more clients. This is going to pay my mortgage, I reminded myself. And I'm helping people. Well, maybe not Ms Hathson, but I had helped most of my other clients so far.

Em had removed all the visible glass shards from both the lounge room and around the window. She had even knocked out the rest of the window glass and taped a sheet over the empty frame.

"I'll get someone in to fix that window after your last client today," she said.

I felt a little dazed as I looked around the freshly tidied lounge room. It amazed me how different she could make a room look in just a few minutes. I would have to ask her to give me some tips some time.

Em had made me a sandwich, which I ate at the kitchen counter. Then I went back to the lounge room to wait for my client. My heart was beating just a little too fast. Please, don't let this be another terrifying session.

Thankfully, the rest of the day's consultations were easy. There were no difficulties in making contact, there was no violence or even threats of it, and no traumatic circumstances. Every client's situation was sad, of course. They only came to me because they had lost someone they loved. Except for Ms Hathson, that is.

Most of my clients wanted confirmation their loved one was in a good place. Some wanted to say things left unsaid. Others wanted to apologise for failures, both real and perceived. And I think most left feeling more at peace, thanking me and gladly handing over my fee.

I was so busy that the week passed quickly. Em and her efficiency became my lifeline, giving me a quiet five minute warning that the client's time was almost up and managing all of my phone calls and messages. Because I was in so much demand, she began scheduling six clients a day and I pushed through my exhaustion by reminding myself that those two extra clients meant another three hundred dollars every day.

Em scheduled a thirty-minute break between each appointment to ensure my clients never came face-to-face with each other. It also gave me time to sit and breathe. Em always had either a snack or a cup of coffee ready for me during those breaks. By the end of her first week, I already didn't know how I had ever coped without her.

TWENTY-SEVEN

Em insisted on a regular meeting with me, so every Friday we sat down at the kitchen counter and she briefed me on interviews and clients for the following week. She also updated me on the state of my finances and carefully tracked the cash and cheques she handled for me. Em was quite the haggler and the payments I received for interviews became noticeably bigger once she took over my business affairs, as she always called them. As for me, I was still struggling to see this as a business. It seemed too easy, despite my constant exhaustion.

By the end of April, Em had worked for me for eight weeks and I was terrified that she would resign. I had asked her to stay on before we even got halfway through her one month trial. We had also increased her hours to six a day, so she usually left around four PM after greeting my second last client for the day.

Em understood the nature of my business by now, of course, although she never asked any questions and didn't display any curiosity about exactly how I communicated with the spirits. Perhaps she assumed I was just as much a fraud as everyone else who claimed to be a speaker. I wondered once or twice whether she might be able to hear the spirits herself. Sometimes she would come into the room when they were there and seem to look around for someone. But if she ever heard anything, she never mentioned it.

She never talked about herself and I still knew next to nothing about her. The only reference to her home life had been that she had some kind of other commitments that kept her busy when she wasn't working for me. I guessed she had a small child – possibly more than one – but I had no other information about her life. I didn't even know how old she was, although I guessed late twenties, or whether she was married. After eight weeks, it seemed a bit late to ask.

Of course, I know far more about her now. There's been many an exposé on her. The *"psychic's" PA* I once saw her referred to as. Sometimes I think people blame her more than they blame me for what happened. Yes, she played her part, but so did I. But that all happened later and I don't want to jump ahead of myself. So, at the end of April, eight weeks after I hired her, Em and I sat at my kitchen counter as she told me about two interviews she had scheduled for the following week.

"And I haven't told you the best news yet."

As always, her facade was entirely professional and gave no indication of what she was about to share.

"Well, tell me then," I said.

"TTM rang yesterday."

I looked at her blankly. "Who? Or what?"

"It's a television station."

"I've never heard of it."

"Are you sure?"

She waited, obviously still expecting me to figure it out. She only gave up when I shrugged at her.

"TTM," she said, "is an American station. It's the home of Sofia."

I didn't have any words for that. Sofia was only the most famous talk show host on American television; possibly the most famous in the world. She had a colossal audience which gave her the power to propel her guests into undreamed of celebrity. I had watched a couple of episodes of her show in those early days after Mac fired me. I never really understood the fascination with her, but I knew she was a big name.

Em's facade cracked and she giggled. My uber-professional assistant actually giggled.

"You fly out for Los Angeles next Saturday. I've moved your appointments for the following week. I had to schedule some for next week — sorry, it does mean you'll have an extra consultation each day — and the rest are re-booked for after you get back. You'll be away for six days. Your flight home leaves LA on a Friday, but with the time zone weirdness, you don't land in Brisbane until Sunday. I've cleared your diary for the Monday, so you can rest after your trip. You'll probably be jetlagged. Actually, we'll probably be jetlagged."

"You're coming with me?" Relief hit me like a wave.

"Of course I am. TTM is paying for flights, accommodation and meals."

When she said how much they were paying for the interview, my jaw dropped.

"They're paying for the trip as well as the interview?"

"Of course," she said. "Their initial offer was just for expenses, but we negotiated."

I would have accepted an offer for expenses for a trip to Los Angeles without a second thought. It probably wouldn't have occurred to me to ask for payment as well and I certainly wouldn't have had the nerve even if I thought of it.

"We're flying first class, by the way," Em added. "Did I mention that yet?"

I shook my head dumbly.

"Right," she said. "That's that. As for next week, like I said, you'll have an extra consultation each day, so it's going to be a big week."

Em was all business again. She briefed me on the week ahead, then checked her watch.

"Twenty minutes until your first client, Dorothy. I'll leave you to prepare."

She scooped up the documents on the counter and whisked them away. There was nothing left for me to do other than wait for my client.

Later, after Em was gone, I told the spirits about my upcoming LA trip.

"Grey, how far do you think you can travel with me?" I asked. "Do you think you will be able to come on the plane? Will LA be too far for you to reach me?"

"I don't know," he said. "Since you don't usually go all that far from home, we've never been able to test how far I can go. I'm not sure that distance really means anything to us here."

"You think you'll be able to find me in LA?"

"I will try," he said. "I will wait for a while after you leave, though. I feel a bit odd about trying to reach you while you're on the plane and you won't be able to talk to me anyway. I'll try to find you in LA a couple of days after you leave. I won't have any way of knowing how much time has passed, though. Remember, the veil is much thicker when you aren't here and we can't see your kitchen clock unless you're around. So if I don't turn up, don't worry. It means I either couldn't go that far or I misjudged the days."

"I hope you can reach me there," I said. "It will feel odd to not be able to talk to any of you. I know the others won't be able to come, but I'll feel better if at least you're there, Gray."

"Remember, we don't think you're supposed to be able to hear us," he said. "I suppose there's a possibility that if you go too far away, our connection might be cut off again."

CHAPTER
TWENTY-EIGHT

With the extra consultations Em had scheduled, the next week flew by. Before I knew it, it was five a.m. on Saturday. Em and I stood on my front deck, bags stacked neatly by the sagging steps, while we waited for a taxi.

I yawned and tried to look more alert than I felt. Getting up at four was the last thing I wanted to do today. But if I lingered after the alarm went off, I would likely go back to sleep and I'd be embarrassed if Em arrived while I was still in bed. She was always so organised that I felt like I had to at least pretend I was semi-organised myself.

So I hauled my weary body out of bed and braced myself with a very strong coffee. I was feeling a little the worse for wear, having polished off an entire bottle of red last night. In a matter of a few months, I had gone from a near teetotaller to drinking a bottle of wine twice a week. It helped me relax in the evening after a long day and I was surprised to discover I liked wine much more than I thought.

Em looked little better than I felt and for the first time, I wondered what effect my busy schedule had on her. I'd never even asked whether she was enjoying the job. I made a mental note to talk to her when I was awake enough to think more clearly.

I wished later I had asked her then while it was on my mind. Perhaps things might have turned out differently. Or perhaps they wouldn't have. I've spent a lot of time wondering whether I could have changed both our stories if I had made the effort to ask right then how she was. But everything's easy in hindsight, isn't it? In reality, when it's five a.m. on Saturday and you've just endured the busiest week of your life, and you're on your way to the airport for your very first international flight, it's all just too hard. Too easy to put off until later.

We left early enough to avoid the usual Saturday morning rush to exit the city for the coast and made it to the airport in less than thirty minutes. Had Em thought of that when she booked our flights? Knowing Em, she had probably considered things that hadn't even occurred to me yet.

We unloaded in the taxi bay and Em went to find a luggage cart while I paid the driver. With our first-class tickets, there was no wait at the check-in counter and ten minutes later, we were left with just our hand luggage. As we passed through security, they pulled Em aside to test her hands for traces of explosive materials. Random screening, apparently, but I wondered whether the Latino tinge in her face was what made them choose her rather than me. Em didn't seem bothered and waited patiently until they cleared her.

In the meantime, I collected our bags from the conveyer belt. Em's battered handbag surprised me. She was always so professional — the ultimate assistant in both appearance and manner — yet her handbag had seen better days. I should buy her a new one, I thought. It would be nice to show her how much I appreciate her.

"Breakfast?" Em suggested. "Or coffee at least? They'll feed us on the plane if you can wait that long."

"Coffee would be good," I agreed.

"Right then." She deposited her handbag and laptop on the closest table. "You wait here."

I piled my own hand luggage on the table and sank into the plastic seat. I was so tired, I could have gone to sleep even sitting in such an uncomfortable chair. Em deposited a couple of coffees on the table and sat opposite me.

"Thanks."

I sipped the coffee with a sigh. It wasn't great coffee, and it could have been hotter, but it helped me to feel a little more human. Once we had finished our coffees, we made our way to the boarding lounge, stopping at a newsagent for Em to purchase some magazines. We settled ourselves in the lounge and I leaned back in my chair, willing myself to stay awake.

"Oh, I forgot about the first-class lounge," Em said some time later. "You can get food and drinks or have a massage or whatever."

"Don't worry about it." My body felt like it had melted into the plastic chair and I couldn't be bothered moving until I had to. "We can check it out on the way home."

Em returned to her magazine and we didn't speak again until our boarding call. The flight was uneventful, although I've got to say that travelling first class is so much nicer than economy. Of course, I've flown first class a few times since then, but on that first trip I felt blessed to have a comfortable seat with a fully reclining back. The hostesses were attentive and the food equivalent to what I would expect in a decent restaurant.

I managed to stay awake until breakfast. Em woke me at dinner time and the next thing I knew we were about to land. The hostesses brought around little warm towels to wipe our faces with. I felt much refreshed by then and ready to deal with whatever the week would bring.

The sight as we flew in over Los Angeles was mind-boggling. With the time zone difference, our mid morning fight got us to LA just before dawn of the same day. The sky was still dark, with just the faintest hint of sunlight peeping over the horizon. The ground was spidered with roads, already congested with the bright headlights of early morning commuters. Between headlights, street lights and house lights, the landscape for as far as I could see in any direction was a mass of white and yellow lights.

We landed at Los Angeles International and I was glad I wasn't alone. It was by far the biggest airport I had ever passed through. It didn't faze Em, though. She led me through baggage claim and immigration, and eventually we emerged into the arrival lounge. Em hesitated, scanning the waiting crowd, then pointed.

"There's our driver."

"They sent a car for us?"

She gave me an odd look.

"Of course they did. They paid for us to fly first class. You think they're going to leave us standing around at the airport?"

I shrugged and didn't reply. Perhaps it was a dumb question, but I was new to all this. I'd never even been out of Australia before, although I had arranged a passport several years ago with the vague intention of travelling one day when I could afford it.

Em spent the drive to our hotel examining my diary. I rarely looked in the book anymore since she kept me up-to-speed and now I saw the pages crammed with her neat handwriting.

"Big week?" I asked.

She gave me a brief, unfocused glance, murmured something vague, and returned to the diary.

Our driver — a skinny Hispanic man in a blue uniform — seemed to speak little English. He was silent and intent on the traffic. With nobody to talk to, I studied the view out the window. There were palm trees everywhere, extending high above the buildings and the power lines, waving in the wind. It gave the city a tropical feeling and despite my fatigue, excitement stirred within me. I was in LA and I was going to be interviewed by Sophia.

TWENTY-NINE

It was almost lunchtime before we reached our hotel in West Hollywood. Em and I had separate rooms right next door to each other. I had expected we would be sharing and felt a surge of gratitude for the unexpected privacy.

"How about we freshen up and I'll come get you in about fifteen minutes?" Em suggested with a glance at her watch. "We can have lunch while I talk you through the week. We have quite a full schedule."

"Sounds fine."

Although I'd slept almost the entire way, I already felt weary. I wasn't sure if I was calculating the time difference correctly, but I thought it was something like five a.m. tomorrow back home. I hung up my pantsuits, hoping the wrinkles would fall out so I wouldn't have to bother ironing. By the time I washed my face and tied my hair back into a ponytail, Em was already knocking on the door.

I suggested going out to find somewhere cheaper than the hotel's own restaurant — after all, the restaurants inside hotels are always ridiculously expensive — but Em shrugged and flashed a debit card.

"Pre-loaded," she said. "We have a food allowance of two hundred and fifty dollars a day."

"That's pretty generous."

When Em had said TTM would pay for meals, I had expected that would mean cheap diners, which was still a level above what I usually ate.

"They think you're hot stuff, Dorothy," Em said.

There was a strangeness to both her face and tone, and I felt a brief pang of fear that she might be considering resigning. Perhaps she hated working for me. Or maybe she begrudged coming along on this trip.

"I'm glad you're here with me," I said, hoping to smooth over whatever the problem was. "I'd hate to be doing this alone."

"Mm," she said. "There's a free table by the window. Let's sit there."

I dismissed her oddness as exhaustion from the flight and from everything she had done to organise this trip so quickly. We sat and a waitress appeared. I ordered a chicken and avocado salad, conscious of the weight I had put on since my original efforts to fit back into my old interview clothes. Em requested a BLT. The waitress disappeared and swiftly returned with our drinks.

We waited in silence for our meals. I fiddled with my glass, making patterns in the condensation on the side. Em stared off into the depths of the restaurant, seemingly lost in thought. She perked up when the food arrived, and as soon as she had finished eating, she reached for my diary.

"Okay, let's run through the week. I won't go into a lot of detail as I'll give you the specifics each morning at breakfast, but I thought it would be useful if you had a sense of the week as a whole."

"Sure," I mumbled around a mouthful of salad.

"Tomorrow morning, Sunday, you have a newspaper interview. The afternoon is free, so if you're feeling any jet lag, you'll be able to sleep it off then. Monday morning you're doing an interview with MBL-TV. Monday afternoon you have the Sofia interview at TTM, which will be filmed in front of an audience. Tuesday morning is an interview with a current affairs program, no audience for that one you'll be pleased to know. Tuesday afternoon is a late night talk show, again filmed with an audience. Wednesday morning a national newspaper. Wednesday afternoon a women's magazine and they'll do a photoshoot after the interview. Thursday afternoon another newspaper, Friday morning a national radio show and a magazine in the afternoon. We fly out late Friday evening. Because of the time difference, it'll be Sunday morning when we arrive home. Your first client is due at nine-thirty on Tuesday."

I had stopped eating about halfway through her list. I knew about the Sofia interview and I figured Em would try to line up one or two others since we were here for a whole week, but I hadn't realised it would be so busy.

"I'm doing interviews all week?"

Em closed the diary with a snap and looked at me.

"Of course. I didn't think you would want to waste time sitting around. At this stage, Thursday morning is free, but I'm expecting that with the buzz from the other interviews, it will fill fast. You might even need to do some evening interviews."

"But—" I felt a little lost for words. "How did you line up so many?"

"When I approached MBL-TV, I only had to mention that you were coming to LA for an interview with Sofia and they couldn't book you fast enough. Then the rest was easy. The talk show rang once word started getting out. The newspaper interviews are unpaid, but they will be great exposure and you're getting paid for everything else. You're making some good money this week, Dorothy. More than a hundred thousand."

I dropped my fork and it clattered to my plate, far too loud in the quiet restaurant.

"A hundred thousand?" I squeaked.

That would pay off more than half my mortgage. I could hardly fathom the change in my luck. Just a couple of months ago, I had been unemployed, broke, and in danger of losing my house.

"US dollars, of course," Em said. "And the exchange rate isn't great right now, but you're going to walk away with something in the vicinity of a hundred and forty thousand Australian. Give or take a few thousand."

"For one week."

Em nodded again, looking at me with an expression I couldn't decipher.

"Em, you have no idea how much I appreciate all your work for this trip."

She nodded and looked down at the diary.

"I'd like to show my appreciation. Let me take you out to dinner tonight. Let's go to one of LA's finest restaurants, the kind celebrities go to. You pick the place. Anywhere you like and dinner's on me."

I thought she would be thrilled, but Em continued to stare down at the diary for another few moments. When she looked up, her face was devoid of expression.

"Thanks, Dorothy, that's a lovely gesture. I'll ask around and make a booking somewhere this afternoon. Now, today is likely to be your only chance to relax. Go take a nap or a swim or whatever. I'll organise a car to pick us up at six."

She flashed me a smile, picked up the diary, and left.

I felt almost rebuffed. Em's words were all correct, but she had shown no enthusiasm. Perhaps I embarrassed her? Or maybe there was something else wrong. Maybe my earlier suspicion that she begrudged accompanying me was correct.

I sighed and went to my room. There was no point agonising over it. When Em was ready to tell me whatever the problem was, we could deal with it. Until then, I'd just be a bit more careful about what I said. The last thing I needed this week was for her to resign and go home. I lay on the bed, too tired to even pull down the covers, and was in a deep sleep when Em knocked on my door.

"Dorothy, are you ready? The car will be here in twenty minutes."

I rolled over and tried to force my eyes to focus on the alarm clock. Five forty-one.

She knocked again. "Dorothy, are you in there?"

I sat up, trying to shake the sleep from my mind.

"Sorry, Em, didn't hear you from the bathroom," I called, hoping I sounded wide awake. "I'm almost ready. Meet you in the lobby?"

I showered and dressed in record time and made it downstairs with two minutes to spare. Em smiled when I arrived and we made small talk in the car on the way to the restaurant. She seemed to be back to her old self over dinner. She had been reading up on the history of LA and gave me a run-down as we ate.

The meal was excellent and the portions so hearty that neither of us could manage dessert. We polished off a bottle of wine, although as we left, I noticed Em's glass was untouched. It hadn't occurred to me to ask whether she wanted wine before I poured her some and there was no way to ask now without sounding nosy.

As we drove back to the hotel, I wondered whether Em would want to go and check out some LA hotspots. It wasn't my sort of thing, but I wouldn't object to tagging along. I opened my mouth to ask, but she looked like she was almost asleep, so I said nothing. When we reached the hotel, we agreed to meet for breakfast at nine, then retreated to our own rooms. House-keeping had been in and had closed the curtains, turned on the bedside lamp and folded down the bed covers.

I pulled off my clothes and crawled into bed, too tired to bother brushing my teeth. I could hear Em moving around her room and talking. Perhaps she had rung her family.

Then I noticed nothing else until a loud ringing woke me. From the brightness of the light streaming in around the curtain, I gathered it was morning. I fumbled for the phone.

"Hello?"

"Ms Marks, this is your wake up call." He sounded ridicu-lously cheerful.

"What time is it?"

"Eight-thirty, ma'am."

"Oh." I pried my eyes open enough to make out the bedside clock. It really was eight-thirty. "Thank you."

"You're most welcome, ma'am."

It would be too easy to roll over and go back to sleep, so I forced myself to sit up. I didn't want to give Em any reason to be peeved at me. Yawning, I tried to calculate the time difference. It was midnight at home, or maybe one a.m. Perhaps that was why I felt like I could have slept for hours yet.

I felt more alive after a shower and with ten minutes to spare before I was supposed to meet Em, I figured I'd head down to the restaurant for a coffee. That way, I might just resemble a functioning human being by the time she arrived.

However, Em was already there, a pot of coffee on the table in front of her. She continued to sip her drink as I poured one for myself. She had smiled when I arrived, but now we sat in silence.

"That feels better," Em said, having drained the last of her coffee. She poured herself another. "Did you sleep well?"

"Surprisingly, yes. I thought the time difference would mess me up, but I guess I was exhausted. You?"

She smiled and nodded but didn't actually answer, instead waving to a waitress who had been hovering nearby. We ordered and the waitress hurried away.

"So," I said to break the silence. "You said last night the interview's at ten, right?"

She nodded. "They're coming here. I've booked a small meeting room within the hotel. Just in case your room is..."

A mess, I knew she was thinking.

"Too small," she finished.

Our food arrived and as with everything she did, Em ate quickly and tidily. She laid the cutlery across her empty plate and folded the napkin neatly on top. I felt a tiny surge of irritation as I looked down at my own plate, which was littered with crumbs and the crusts of my toast. It wasn't fair that Em was so good at everything.

The interview went well. The journalist, Ben, had done his research. He asked some unusually insightful questions, not just the typical "can you see the ghosts too or just hear them". The interview went for more than an hour and Ben looked pleased as he wrapped up.

"I'm hoping to finish this in time for tomorrow's deadline," he told me as he shook my hand. "We'd like to capitalise on your TV appearances with an article in Tuesday's edition."

"That sounds lovely."

I had a feeling it wasn't the most appropriate response, but I was always at a loss as to what to say to something like that. Em intervened before I could make a further fool of myself.

"Ben, will you let me know when you know for sure what

day it will be printed?" she asked. "You have my contact details. An email will be fine."

Ben agreed and left.

"I think that went well," I said.

Em nodded, her face blank, and glanced at her watch.

"The rest of the day is clear. Do you need anything from me?"

I had been going to suggest we have lunch and do some sightseeing together, but it seemed Em had her own plans.

"No, I'm still feeling jet-lagged, so I might have a nap."

It wasn't true, but I wanted her to feel free to leave me alone if that was what she wanted.

"Great," she said. "I will head off then. I'll probably see you tonight, but if not, I need you in the lobby tomorrow at six a.m., okay? You'll get a wake-up call at five-thirty. Your interview with MBL-TV is scheduled for nine and they need you to go through hair and makeup first."

"What should I wear?"

"I'd suggest the red dress. You brought that, didn't you?"

I tried to remember what had ended up in my suitcase.

"I think so."

"They'll check your clothes when we get there anyway, so you don't need to worry too much. They'll find you something else if necessary. Make sure the colours are right for TV, that sort of thing."

She left then, off to do her own thing. Sightseeing, I presumed, or shopping. Making the most of a free trip over-seas. Whatever. She was entitled to some time off. I would need to ensure I paid her for this morning since she didn't usually work weekends. And she would be working longer hours each day this week. I would have to tell her to keep track of her hours so I could pay her accordingly. Perhaps that would resolve her problem. She was probably disgruntled that I hadn't already offered to pay her for the extra time while we were away. I was pleased I'd solved the mystery. Once Em knew I would pay her in full, she'd be back to her usual self.

I decided to relax by the pool for a while and make the most of the beautiful spring weather. I swapped my interview attire for some comfy shorts and a t-shirt. There were only two people at the pool, so I went to the opposite end and settled in with my e-reader. I had difficulty getting into my book, though, knowing I'd be unlikely to finish it while I was away. Mostly, I just sat and watched the way the sunlight sparkled on the water.

After lunch, I bought a guidebook from the hotel book store and went to do some sightseeing. Half a day wasn't enough time to see LA, but if I could only do one thing, I knew what it would be: Rodeo Drive. The street where Julia Roberts is refused service in *Pretty Woman* and later returns to show the snotty saleswoman the error of her ways. "Big mistake," she says, hefting her bags of goodies from other stores. "Huge." I love that scene.

I wandered along Rodeo Drive, marvelling at the extravagance on display, then spent the rest of the afternoon exploring Hollywood Boulevard. Hollywood was something of a shock. It was not the glitzy, glamorous place I had anticipated. Sure, there was a block or two that was clean and sparkly, filled with tourists, space troopers and Wonder Woman, but venture outside of that area and it became quieter and grubbier. Cigarette shops replaced the souvenir shops and the carefully made-up and smiling shop assistants became skinny Hispanic men who lingered on the footpath and smoked.

I clutched my handbag, nervous of being mugged, as I followed the Walk of Fame past the dingy shops. Eventually, I turned back and returned to the more vibrant part of the street. Having seen the Kodak Theatre, Graubman's and the Hollywood Wax Museum, I headed back to the hotel for a solitary dinner and an early night.

As I lay in bed, my stomach churned with nerves at the prospect of my first live television interview. Sleep was a long time coming as I imagined all the ways I might make a fool of myself on American TV. I hoped Gray might arrive before I went to sleep, but he didn't. Perhaps I was too far away after all.

CHAPTER

THIRTY

I was already awake when the phone rang promptly at five-thirty for my wake up call. I took my time showering, inhaling the soap-scented steam while I tried to steady my nerves. It didn't work and by the time I was dressed, my hands were shaking. I gave my hair a quick brush but didn't bother tying it back or putting on any makeup. The makeup artist would probably undo whatever I did, anyway. I wasn't terribly proficient at anything more than mascara and I had a vague notion that applying makeup for television was different to applying it for normal wear. Something to do with the lights, I supposed.

I was in the lobby by ten to six. Em was, of course, already there, dressed in a neat navy suit. She carried a large folder and her laptop and looked every inch the professional.

"Good morning, Dorothy," she said. "How are you feeling?"

"Nervous. My stomach is doing backflips."

"Here, have one of these." Em fished in her handbag and retrieved a roll of antacids. "It might settle your stomach."

"Thanks."

I popped one into my mouth just as the front doors opened.

A very large black man wearing an immaculate suit and an ear piece entered. After a swift look around the lobby, he headed our way.

"Ms Marks?" he said. "I'm Chuck. I've come from MBL-TV with your car."

Chuck led us out to a long black sedan with dark tinted windows. He opened the door, waited until we were both settled in the back, then got into the front passenger seat. I had assumed he was our driver.

"Hi, I'm Mark," the guy in the driver's seat said.

Em and I introduced ourselves as Mark pulled the car out into the traffic.

"So, Chuck, what do you do with MBL-TV?" Em asked.

I felt a little less daft that she, too, must have assumed he was our driver.

"Security." He flipped down the sun visor so he could see us in the mirror on the back. "We have something of a situation at the studio today."

"A situation?" Em and I spoke together.

"What sort of situation?" she asked.

Chuck studied us in the mirror, his jaw working as he decided what to tell us.

"A group of protestors," he said.

I relaxed back into my seat. Nothing for me to worry about then. The network must have sent Chuck as a precaution.

"What sort of protestors?" Em asked, holding his gaze in the mirror.

He cleared his throat and looked away out the window.

"Group of Christians."

"Protesting about Dorothy?" she asked.

I frowned. "Why on earth would Christians be protesting about me? I haven't done anything to them. I haven't even said anything about them."

Chuck kept his face blank and stared out the window as he spoke.

"Ma'am, if half of what I've read about you is true, it's what you do they're worried about, not so much what you say."

Em, as usual, grasped the core of the matter instantly.

"Dorothy, what you've done is shown that one of the cornerstones of their religion is a lie."

I didn't know whether to be indignant or horrified.

"I've done no such thing. I've never made any public comment about religion. Any religion."

"Don't you get it?" Em's professional veneer cracked and a hint of exasperation showed through. "Christians believe that when we die, we go off to heaven or paradise or whatever you want to call it. You've shown that what really happens, for some of us at any rate, is that we linger here somewhere. If people can't rely on their beliefs about what happens after death, what does that mean for the rest of their ideology? What you do shatters everything they believe in. Of course, they want to silence you."

"Silence me?" My stomach rolled. "They wouldn't try to do anything, would they?"

I directed my question at Em, but she looked towards Chuck and waited for his response.

"That's what I'm here for, ma'am." He sounded unbothered. "We're not expecting trouble, but protestors of any kind can be unpredictable. You just need to follow my instructions and everything will be fine. As we come up to the studio, we'll slow down to drive through the crowd. We stay in the car until we get inside the fence. Security will lock the gates after us and then we're clear."

"See, Dorothy, Chuck has it all under control." Em gave me a look I couldn't read.

We passed the rest of the drive in silence. The car slowed as we approached a large building with a prominent MBL-TV sign. It stood behind a set of tall, wrought-iron gates. About a dozen protestors waited in front of them. I had imagined a rowdy mob of hundreds, but this group seemed to be standing around silently. There were a few placards on sticks, but no weapons. I felt a surge of relief. It wasn't nearly as bad as I had pictured. As the car approached, the protesters turned towards us.

Someone yelled, "Is that her?"

"Should be here about now," someone else shouted. "I think that's her."

They ran towards the car and my heart beat hard enough to burst right through my chest. I glanced at Chuck in the mirror, but he looked almost bored. That didn't make me feel any better. He probably did this every day and besides, it wasn't him they wanted. The car slowed and I jumped as the doors locked with a loud click.

"No need for alarm, Ms Marks." Chuck eyeballed me from the mirror. "It's just a precaution. They're unlikely to try to get in, but there's no sense in not locking the doors."

I nodded, my mouth too dry to respond. I wanted to tell the driver to keep going and get me far away from here. The protestors crowded close, peering in through the windows, but nobody touched the car. They held up the placards as if wanting me to read them. *Heaven Is Real and So Is Hell. Repent While There Is Time. Ghost-speaking Is From the Devil. Jesus Will Raise Us Up.*

"They think I'm evil." I didn't know how to interpret my reaction. I felt confused. Irritated, bordering on anger. Amused. But mostly just bewildered.

"Pay them no attention, Ms Marks," Chuck said. "They do it to get a rise out of you. If you ignore them, they'll likely be long gone before you leave."

I jumped as a protestor knocked on the window.

"Repent, Dorothy." He peered in through the tinted glass.

His wiry hair stuck out around his head, giving him a wild appearance, and his eyes were frighteningly intense. He kept pace with the slow crawl of the car. "Repent while you can. Ask Jesus to remove the spawn of Satan from your heart. Let him wash your sins away."

I averted my eyes, staring down at my hands, which were clasped in my lap and trembling just a little. We reached the gates and the car stopped. The man continued to stare through the window as the gates opened. We drove through and Mark stopped the car beside a blue door.

"There you go, Ms Marks." Chuck sounded almost cheerful. "Delivered safe and sound. You should be fine heading back, but I'll ride with you, just in case."

As I left the car, I was acutely aware of the protestors staring at me from the other side of the gates. They were quiet now, although I convinced myself I could feel hatred rolling off them. By the time we were out of the car, a woman in a beige suit waited at the door. She looked to be in her thirties and was smartly dressed, with her hair pinned back in a smooth bun. I felt underdressed and dishevelled next to her.

"Welcome to MBL-TV," she said, giving us a practiced smile. She held the door open and gestured for us to enter. "If we could hurry, please. You're a little later than I expected."

"Traffic was bad," the driver muttered, but she seemed to pay him no attention.

"I'm Julie Hawkins," she said as she swept us inside. "Executive assistant to Lorenzo Garcia who will be producing the show this morning."

I smiled a hello, but of course it was Em who offered her hand and introduced herself. My cheeks reddened, but I figured I'd look even more socially inept if I did the same now. Julie whisked us down the hallway. I was already rattled by the protestors, but as I sat in front of a brightly lit mirror while the makeup artist worked on me, I became increasingly nervous. By the time they sent me to the green room, where Em was sipping a coffee, I was ready to vomit.

Em said later that I spoke well in the interview and my nerves weren't apparent. Thankfully, the journalist didn't ask about the protestors as I wouldn't have had a clue what to say. Perhaps he hadn't been briefed on what was happening outside, or perhaps he just didn't think it was appropriate for morning TV. Chuck was waiting in the green room afterwards to escort us back to the car. I wondered what the driver thought of Em's request to take us to TTM for the Sophia interview rather than back to the hotel, but he just shrugged as if to say it was all the same to him.

Being interviewed by Sofia was the most surreal experience I've ever had. I've been interviewed by plenty of big names since then, but she was the first and still the biggest. The studio audience went crazy every time Sofia so much as looked in their direction, which added to my overwhelm.

By the time a TTM car dropped us back to the hotel, I was exhausted and starving. Em had eaten breakfast in the green room at MBL-TV and lunch at TTM, but I had been too nervous to even look at the food.

"Shall we eat in the hotel restaurant?" Em asked, as I tried to stifle an enormous yawn. I nodded, unable to speak through my yawn, and she checked her watch. "It's almost five. Why don't you go upstairs and nap for an hour, then we'll eat."

Em obviously had her own plans for that hour as she stayed in the lobby while I stumbled off to the lift. I let myself into my room with a sigh and wondered whether to bother with a shower or just collapse into bed.

"Hi, Dorothy."

If I hadn't been so out of it, I would have sensed Gray's presence before he spoke.

"Gray. I thought I must be too far away."

"I guess not."

"I'm pleased you're here." And I was. He was a security blanket amid all this madness. "It's pretty crazy here."

"What's happened?" He sounded like he was settling in for a chat.

I tried to stifle another yawn.

"Geez, I'm sorry, Gray. I'm just too beat to talk at the moment. Can we talk when I get back from dinner tonight?"

"Sure. You look like you could do with some rest."

I was already crawling into bed and yawned again.

"I'm glad you're here, Gray."

If he made any reply, I was already fast asleep and didn't hear.

THIRTY-ONE

I never did get a chance to talk to Grey that evening. After dinner, I went back to my room and straight to bed. I somehow fell asleep again after my wake up call on Tuesday and didn't stir until Em had reception call me a second time. I threw on some clothes and rushed down to the lobby, where Em was already halfway through a pot of coffee.

That breakfast was the last moment of peace we had on the trip because once the Sofia interview aired later that day, Em's phone rang constantly. She scheduled last-minute interviews for the evenings, one after tomorrow morning's interview, and three for Thursday morning. There was even one for the hour before we needed to leave for the airport on Friday.

"Are you sure we can fit all these in?" I asked on the way to a talk show interview on Tuesday.

"It's a tight schedule and we can't afford to fall behind, but it should be fine," she said. "I'll cancel something if it becomes too much. Probably one of the newspaper interviews, since they're just about the only ones that don't pay."

Em kept her gaze out the window. Not that there was much to see from the highway. Just lanes of concrete and traffic, and palm trees. Palm trees everywhere. It would be my enduring image of LA.

I wanted to ask how much she had negotiated for all those extra interviews, but not in front of the driver. My stomach churned as we pulled up outside a large grey complex plastered with the MoMoTV signs. The constant feeling of nausea was becoming all too familiar. If I had been relieved that my previous interviews didn't mention the protestors, I should have expected that Rick Firman wouldn't go easy on me.

"So Dorothy," he said as we sat on comfortable armchairs on the stage. I could hear rustling and whispering from the audience, but they were almost invisible behind the bright stage lights. "You caused quite a sensation when you appeared at MBL-TV."

"That was a lot of fun."

"I hear there was a protest outside the studio when you arrived."

I chose my words with care. Em and I had discussed what I should say if anyone asked about the protesters, but Rick was the first to do so.

"There was a small group of protestors."

"Are you aware of what they were protesting about?"

I must have had a stricken look on my face because he relented a little.

"They were protesting about you," he said.

"Me?" It was easy to sound shocked.

"There are some Americans who think what you do must be straight from Satan."

"How can you say that? I give peace to people. They get a chance to say the things they didn't say before. And, likewise, the spirit who has passed has a final opportunity to say what they need to. It gives my clients an enormous sense of relief and peace. How can you possibly think that is satanic?"

"Some Christians feel that your words must be lies. That you don't really communicate with the dead. Because if you do, it means their belief that the faithful go to heaven after death must be wrong."

"Maybe they don't go straight to heaven. Perhaps there is an intermediate stop on the way, a place where people can seek closure for any unfinished business from their lives."

"Some Christians believe your claim to speak to spirits is an attempt by Satan to bamboozle them, to make them believe there is no heaven."

"I don't know whether or not there's a heaven." I felt trapped. "How can I answer that?"

"Have you ever asked any of the spirits with whom you communicate whether there is a heaven?"

"Of course not."

"Why not?"

"What's the point in distressing them? I don't know whether they have any memory of the fact that they might have thought they were supposed to be on their way to heaven. What purpose would it serve to remind them? I'm trying to help people. Nothing more."

"So you don't believe your ability to speak to spirits is a gift from the devil?"

"Of course not." Hadn't I already answered that?

"Where does this ability come from then?"

"I have no idea."

"Have you always been able to communicate with the dead?"

That question had been asked repeatedly and I had my answer down pat by now.

"I don't know whether I've always been able to. It's an ability I came to a gradual awareness of."

"What was it like as a child to know you heard things that other children didn't?"

"I don't have a lot of memory about that," I said. "I don't remember at what age I first realised what I could do but, like I said, it was a gradual realisation. To me, it's never seemed strange or unnatural. It's just an ability I have and I'm trying to use that ability to help people as much as I can."

"Well, Dorothy, why don't we try out that ability of yours right now?"

"What do you mean?"

"Let's call up a member of the audience and see if you can connect them with a lost loved one."

Rick seemed to find the look on my face amusing as he turned back to the audience.

"Now, as you can see, Dorothy wasn't expecting this request. She has in no way been briefed about this. I'm going to select a member of the audience to take part in our experiment. Who would like to help us out?"

Hands shot up in the air and there was an immediate clamour. Rick pointed.

"You there, lady in the orange top, third row from the front. Who have you lost?"

"My mother."

The glare of the stage lights obscured my view of the woman. I had an impression of dark hair, but that was about it.

"And how long ago was that?" Rick asked.

"Almost three years."

"Well, Dorothy." Rick turned back to me. "What do you think? Do you have any sort of criteria we need to fill?"

"No, not at all." I hoped my voice didn't betray my nerves. Dear lord, please don't let this turn out to be like the lightbulb-shattering incident.

Rick turned back to the woman. "Okay, love, just for the record, have you ever had any contact with Dorothy?"

"No, I haven't."

"And have any of our staff briefed you before our session here today?"

"No."

"Right, Dorothy, do your stuff."

He leaned back in his chair. I couldn't read the look on his face, but I was pretty sure he expected me to fail.

"I have a couple of questions for her first," I said. "I need to know who I'm trying to contact."

"Ask away," he said.

"What is your first name?" I asked, directing my question to the woman I couldn't see.

"Gabby," came the reply.

"Gabby, what was your mother's name?"

"Gloria. Gloria Jacobs."

"And how old was Gloria when she died?"

"Fifty-five. She—"

"No details," I said. "Please."

I took a deep breath and closed my eyes. This moment would make or break me. My heart thudded. My hands were sweaty and I clasped them in my lap in case their trembling was visible on camera. Thank goodness I already knew Grey could reach me here. I could only hope he would hear me now.

"Speak to me, spirits. I'm seeking contact with Gloria Jacobs, aged fifty-five."

My voice wobbled a little, making me even more nervous. I couldn't sense Gray yet.

"Just a minute, Dorothy." Gray sounded as calm and confident as ever. "I think she's here."

I've never been so relieved to hear his voice or feel his presence. I waited with my eyes closed, painfully aware of the shuffling and mumblings from the audience. They didn't think I could do it. They thought I was a fraud. Gray relayed the spirit's words and we fell into our accustomed routine. I soon forgot about the audience.

"Gabby, your mother says hello to Gabby-Bear. She says she's sorry she didn't tell you about the breast cancer earlier. She thought you had enough to deal with after the miscarriage and the divorce without knowing about her diagnosis."

There was a collective intake of breath from the audience.

"She didn't tell you when she went through the first two rounds of chemo. She's never forgiven herself for not telling you until she knew there was no chance of her survival. She thinks you would have dealt better with her death if you had more time to prepare for it. You've always meant the world to her, especially since she could never bear any other children after you. She's sorry she left you alone and hopes you can forgive her. Gabby, she wants you to move on with your life and find someone new to love. And she wants you to know that more than anything, she loves you."

It was only through practice that I kept my voice steady. Every communication was emotional and over the months I had learnt not to let my emotions come out during the consultation. There have been plenty of occasions, though, when I cried after the client left. Today I had to keep it together until I got back to the hotel.

"That's all, Gabby. I've lost her now."

I opened my eyes, blinking against the harshness of the stage lights. The audience was still and silent.

"Well." Rick cleared his throat. "That was very... specific. Gabby, what's your reaction?"

I could hear her sobbing. No wonder the audience had gone so quiet. I hadn't noticed when that happened, but they must be able to see what I couldn't. It took several minutes for Gabby to stop crying enough to speak. Someone off to the side of the stage motioned to Rick, telling him to wrap up, and he gave a dismissive flick of the hand, barely noticeable if you weren't watching carefully.

"It's all true," Gabby said eventually. "Every word she said. My mother died of breast cancer and she didn't tell me until the doctors ran out of options. She had been through two rounds of chemo by then. My husband and I had separated and I had a miscarriage just a few weeks later. I didn't even know I was pregnant. That was just before her diagnosis."

"Gabby, are you an only child?" Rick's voice was as steady and professional as ever, but his face showed his amazement. He hadn't expected me to pass his test.

Another sob. "When my mother went into labour, there were complications. She had to have an emergency caesarean and a hysterectomy. I grew up telling her how much I wanted a brother or sister and it must have broken her heart every time."

The murmurs from the audience swelled into a clamour of people demanding I contact spirits for them next. Rick cocked an eyebrow at me and I shook my head.

"No more," I whispered, hoping the microphone wouldn't pick it up.

Rick nodded and turned back to the audience.

"There you have it. Dorothy Marks, the clairvoyant from Australia who has been lauded as the real deal has just demonstrated her talents on national television. And I'll say it again, Dorothy had no idea I was going to ask her to do that today."

He stood and shook my hand, then an assistant was at my side to show me which direction to leave in. Em waited in the green room. From the look on her face, I knew she'd been watching the interview on the TV screen in there. She didn't look happy about it, though. Perhaps because the consultation hadn't been agreed ahead of time. She probably would have wanted to negotiate a higher payment if she knew they expected a consultation as well as an interview.

We walked to the waiting car in silence. I stumbled along, oblivious to everything else and trying to keep myself together. I didn't want anyone, least of all Em, to see me break down. Em's phone rang not two minutes into our drive. I felt her hesitation as she looked at it.

"It's all right." I kept my gaze fixed on the window and willed the tears in my eyes not to fall. "Go ahead."

I only half listened to her conversation, although I would have preferred not to overhear it. Em said little other than that she would put a proposal to me and get back to the caller. She hung up and the phone rang again. She finished the second call just as we pulled into the hotel and switched her phone to silent.

"Dorothy, we need to talk."

"Can it wait, Em?" I asked with a sigh.

The constant phone calls could only mean one thing — more work — and right now, I couldn't face anything. I wanted to go up to my room, crawl into bed, and bawl.

She frowned at me. "Not really. We should discuss this. The phone is only going to keep ringing once I turn it back on."

"So don't turn it on." I was too busy concentrating on keeping myself together to care if I sounded rude. "Just give me a couple of hours."

I was already heading into the hotel. Em didn't follow and I didn't look back to see her reaction. Perhaps I should have.

THIRTY-TWO

G ray arrived as I entered my room and his presence was like a favourite blanket, familiar and soothing. I closed the door and flung myself onto the bed. He didn't speak until my tears slowed.

"I know, Dorothy. That was a tough one."

His sympathy set me off again and I bawled for another few minutes. When I finally stopped, I sat up and reached for the tissue box.

"Do you still feel things the same way?" I asked. "Emotions."

"Sometimes. It's hard to explain. Things that happen on the other side of the veil are kind of separate from us. Seeing or hearing something that would have upset us once doesn't have the same effect unless it's someone we're linked to. That contact was difficult for Gloria. Her daughter's distress hit her hard."

"So when something upsets me, it affects you too?"

"Yes."

I waited, but he said nothing further.

"Who are you, Gray?" My inability to identify him had never been more frustrating. "Who are you to me?"

I felt his presence dim, as if he was leaving. I had broken one of their rules again. But then he returned.

"I don't know," he said, but his voice was different now. Distant. "Where you go, I go. When you hurt, I feel it. I wondered..."

"What? If you've got any clue, please tell me."

"I wondered whether there might have been something between us once. Maybe you were an ex-girlfriend. Someone I was still in love with when I died."

"I'm sorry, Gray. I've never dated anyone with your name."

"What if that's not my name?"

"You don't think it is?" Could he be Gary after all?

"I don't know. Maybe Gray means something else to me. It could be someone I knew once. Maybe I've forgotten my name and Gray is a reference to something else, something that held particular significance for me."

"Oh, Gray, I wish I could tell you I knew who you are and what your connection to me is. I only have a couple of former boyfriends and I don't think anyone has died. The only person who might be linked to me is my brother."

"Gary." Again, his voice was distant.

"Yes, Gary. I don't know whether or not to hope that you're him."

He didn't answer, reminding me of the way he had acted after I had asked to speak to Gary that time. Gray had said they couldn't find him, but what if that wasn't true? What if Gray really was Gary and he didn't remember or he just didn't want to tell me?

"Gray, I don't know what our connection is, but I couldn't imagine not having you around."

"It's not like I'm going anywhere." He spoke before I could

apologise for my thoughtless comment. "It's okay. This is my problem, not yours. I don't know why I'm tied to you, but if I can figure it out, maybe I can move on."

Was the other side of the veil the last stop for all spirits? When I died, would I join my spirit friends in that strange place? Or was there something else for some people? It felt awful to hope there was, as if I was condemning my friends to live forever in this godless place they had found themselves.

"Do you think there's more to the afterlife? More than what's there on the other side of the veil?"

"I hope so. Now why don't you get some rest? I'll stay while you sleep."

I was almost asleep when I thought of one more thing I wanted to ask.

"Grey? If you move on, I won't be able to speak with you anymore, will I?"

He sighed. "Honestly, Dorothy, I don't know. We don't think we're supposed to have this connection with you and it wasn't there when you first moved into the house. We don't know what made us suddenly able to reach you and we don't know how long it will last."

CHAPTER

THIRTY-THREE

I had lost track of the days, but whatever today was, Em would have it crammed full of interviews. She was already waiting in the restaurant when I went down for breakfast and by the time I reached the table, she had the diary open. Even the margins were filled with notes.

"Looks like I need a day-to-a-page diary these days rather than that old one," I said, reaching for the coffeepot.

Of course, Em didn't know I'd bought the week-to-a-page at Bec's request. She frowned down at the diary.

"That would be useful. This isn't particularly."

"Em, I'm sorry about last night."

Her jaw clenched and she sighed. For a moment, I thought she would actually tell me what bothered her.

"Don't worry about it," she said. "You were exhausted, especially after Rick's surprise request. We're both worn out and I don't know about you, but I'm starving. Shall we order?"

She was already waving the waitress over. As the woman left, Em closed the diary and put it to one side.

"There are some things we need to discuss," she said. "My phone kept ringing last night until I switched it off around midnight. I haven't turned it on yet today and I'm almost afraid to find out how many messages I have."

"Were they all wanting interviews?"

"It's bigger than that. I had calls from agents — entertainment agents — who want to represent you. I stopped counting how many. There were also seven calls from people who want to manage you. I had requests for interviews from all over North America and Australia as well as England, France, Germany, Austria—" She opened the diary again to check her notes. "Italy, Spain, two from China, one from Thailand, and one from Russia."

"Somebody in Russia has heard of me?"

Em just looked at me.

"What do I do?" I asked.

"There are some decisions you need to make. First, do you want to consider a manager or an agent or both?"

"I don't know. What do they do?"

"A manager organises your appointments and your diary. They liaise with people on your behalf, arrange your travel, follow up to make sure you get paid, that sort of stuff."

"All the things you do."

Her face didn't change. "Yes."

"So what would you do if I hired a manager?"

She looked down at the diary. It took a couple of heartbeats before I realised.

"Oh, Em, I'm sorry. I didn't mean it that way. Of course I wouldn't give you up. I couldn't function without you."

"You wouldn't need me if you had a manager."

"Don't be ridiculous. Of course I would. But why can't you be my manager?"

"Because you don't pay me enough."

"Oh. Of course. If I increased your pay, would you be my manager?"

"Dorothy, it's not a job that can be done in thirty hours a week. You need a full-time manager, someone who is available weekends and evenings when necessary. I don't know whether I could make myself available. If that's what you're offering."

"Of course it is. How much does a manager make?"

She shrugged. "I don't know."

"Okay then, find out. I'll pay you whatever the industry standard is."

Em looked at me. "Like I said, I have other commitments."

"Plus twenty per cent."

"I'll consider it."

I supposed that was all I could ask. After all, there was the child to consider. At least, I assumed it was a child that formed her other commitments. She was very private about her personal life, and respecting that, I never asked.

"Good. In the meantime, you can tell anyone who asks about managing me that I've already made an offer. So what else was there?"

"Agents. I stopped counting how many."

"What is the difference between an agent and a manager?"

"A manager receives a salary and an agent gets a percentage of what you earn from the bookings they negotiate for you. An agent wouldn't manage your day-to-day appointments, just the interviews. If you have a manager, I don't think you need an agent for Australia, but it might be worth considering one for the overseas markets. Someone with good contacts. An agent for North America would certainly be useful right now. They could field all these phone calls and only pass on the best offers."

"And they would earn a portion of those offers."

"Yes, but you would also expect them to negotiate bigger payments than I can get you."

Our meals arrived and I buttered my toast. Em ignored hers and continued to study the diary.

"I don't know," I said. "Let me think about it."

"Fine." She made a note in the diary. "Okay, tours. Are you open to the idea of touring? We could book you to do appearances all over North America. I'm hearing some very big figures tossed around."

To be honest, I wasn't interested. This week had been too busy. I was exhausted, both mentally and physically, and the thought of doing this for weeks on end was way too much.

"How big?"

"Several million. For an eight-week tour around North America, I'm hearing amounts in the range of three to six million."

"Three million dollars for eight weeks?"

Maybe I was interested after all.

"At least. Keep in mind this is just initial offers, which nobody would expect you to take. I think you could expect to double that."

Six million, maybe more, for eight weeks. How could I say no to that, no matter what it might do to me? Eight weeks and I'd be set for life. I'd never have to worry about looking for a job if the spirit work dried up. I'd never have to worry about money again. Ever.

"Let's check it out," I said. "See what sort of offers you can get. For that sort of money, I'd be crazy to say no."

CHAPTER

THIRTY-FOUR

Before I knew it, we were on the plane and heading home. I was so exhausted that I slept the entire way. Em was staring out the window when I went to sleep and was still doing the same thing when I woke for breakfast. It was almost noon by the time I let myself into the house. I had never been so pleased to be home.

I dragged my bags upstairs and left them on the floor in the bedroom. It was beyond me to even think about unpacking. I had barely enough left in me to shower and crawl into bed. I had only just started adjusting to the time zone difference when we left LA. It was the middle of the afternoon back there, and despite my fatigue, I couldn't sleep.

It had been a very good week. Offers were still coming in thick and fast. Em hadn't given me a decision yet about being my manager and I didn't push her. She was still acting odd and I had no idea why. My offer to pay her for all the time she worked while we were away didn't seem to have helped. Perhaps she missed home and her family. Or maybe she begrudged going to LA with me. But it wasn't like I asked her to go — she was the one who had arranged it all.

I hadn't been joking when I said I wouldn't know what to do without her. She made everything run so smoothly that I couldn't imagine doing it all by myself again. I'd have to hire someone else if she decided not to be my manager, but nobody else could do the job the way Em did.

The spirits were waiting when I woke up and they seemed pleased to have me home. I had missed Bec, Lissa and Samson and was relieved to find them all just the same. I had been half afraid they mightn't be here when I got back or that our connection might have been lost like Gray had warned before I left.

Bec, a strange mix of bossy and maternal, clucking around her little tribe like a mother hen. The quickest to take offence and the slowest to get over it, but always there when I needed her, even if she made me work for it.

Lissa was cheery and often air-headed. Always eager to help, although we didn't let her take part in my appointments. In some ways, I suppose that was daft. She was dead, after all. Life doesn't get much more confronting than that. Like the others, she never said anything about how she had died, but I suspected she had been murdered. There was always accident and misadventure, but the taint of murder seemed to hang around her like a smoky cloud.

Samson was still the one I knew the least. He worshipped Lissa and the two of them were rarely apart. In life, they would make an odd couple, a middle-aged black man hanging around with a white teenaged girl. It was the sort of pairing that would raise both eyebrows and suspicions in most company. Was their friendship critiqued on the other side of the veil the way it would be here? Or did we leave those biases behind with our physical lives?

And, of course, there was Gray. I'd had little time to speak to him since the Rick Firman interview, but if I woke in the middle of the night, he was usually there, as if watching over me while I slept. In the sea of craziness that had somehow become my life, he was a solid anchor.

At first they were a rowdy, intrusive group of spirits that happened to cohabit the house I had presumed I lived in alone. Then I got to know them and they became my friends. In fact, they seemed to have somehow become my family.

It was an unfamiliar experience for me. I had never been close to either my parents or my brother, although Gary had been making efforts to get closer in the year or two before his death. I had rebuffed him, though. Too busy with work, too tired when I wasn't at work, and it just didn't seem important to establish a relationship with my brother. As children, we squabbled incessantly and we had carried that over into our adult relationship, perhaps more out of habit than any genuine disagreement. It is only in hindsight that you wish you'd spent the time to get to know someone. I wondered sometimes whether the petty fights and quibbles could have been resolved if I knew him better. Could we have been friends, my younger brother and I?

The more I thought about it, I didn't think that Gray could be Gary. Gray seemed nothing like my brother, either in voice or personality. I was both disappointed and relieved. Disappointed I hadn't found the answer Gray was searching for, but relieved it wasn't Gary stuck on the other side of the veil. Perhaps he was one of those spirits who didn't linger. Or perhaps he had moved on to whatever awaited a spirit once all of their earthly business was complete. Or maybe there was no afterlife for some of us.

CHAPTER
THIRTY-FIVE

"I had an interesting phone call this morning," Em said, as we sat at my kitchen table a couple of weeks later. Life had returned to its usual routine except that my phone rarely rang anymore since Em had set up a website for me with her phone number on it.

She was booking clients six months in advance and even had a wait list of people she would call on one of the very rare occasions that a client cancelled. She had eventually agreed to become my manager and now worked for me full time. I didn't ask how she had resolved her other commitments and she, as usual, didn't volunteer any information.

"Define interesting," I said, buttering my toast. Breakfast wasn't my favourite time to meet with Em, but it had become the most practical.

"Interesting as in out of the ordinary and weird. I'm not sure what to make of it."

I bit into my toast. Life was too busy these days to hesitate on the chance to eat.

"It was David Evans," she said.

That got my attention mid-crunch. "*The* David Evans? The hot-shot American psychic?"

"Biggest psychic in the world, or so he tells me."

"What did he want?"

"To meet you if you go back to the US. Apparently, the Rick Firman interview caught his attention."

I choked on my toast and spent the next few minutes sipping my coffee and banging myself on the chest. Em waited, studying her new day-to-a-page diary. I felt Lissa arrive, likely coming to see what all my coughing and hacking was about. She didn't speak though — the spirits rarely did when Em was around. I didn't miss the way Em glanced over her shoulder, though, at Lissa's arrival.

"Are you okay?" Em asked when my coughs eventually subsided.

I felt as if I had hacked up a lung in the process of trying to dislodge the rogue crumbs.

"I'm fine. David Evans wants to meet me? Why?"

Em hesitated. "That's what I'm not sure about. Perhaps he's just checking out the competition. Maybe he has a proposal for you."

"I'm hardly competition for David Evans. He has his own talk show, regular world tours, the works. He sells out twenty thousand seat venues. I'm just—"

"The newest psychic in town," she interrupted. "And right now, his biggest competition. You know we've got offers for tours through North America and Europe. It wouldn't take much to kick off a feeding frenzy. You would be booked solid for TV appearances all the way. I think you could get your own talk show if you wanted it. You would have to move to the US, though. LA probably."

I shook my head.

"Your faith in me always amazes me. Listening to you, I can

almost believe I'm David Evans' biggest competition. But when you stop talking, I remember who I am: Dorothy Marks, a chick from Brisbane who only got into the spirit business because she lost her job."

"I can never understand why you don't take any pride in what you do." Em's eyes flashed as she closed the diary with a snap. "You bring peace to so many people. And when you decide on these tour offers, you're going to be a multi-million-aire, if you're not already. Have you realised that?"

She had mentioned expecting to negotiate at least six million for the multitude of interviews that would comprise a tour, but I hadn't thought of it in those terms before. Me, a multi-millionaire?

"I always feel like I don't deserve all the attention," I confessed. "After all, I don't do anything. I just sit back and wait for the spirits to talk, then say whatever they tell me. There's no talent involved. Nothing that feels like hard work. I sit in an armchair all day, for crying out loud."

"So you're saying anyone could do what you do?"

Em gave me a look I was familiar with. She used it when-ever she thought I was being daft, which seemed to be often.

"Well, yes, provided they had the contacts that I do."

"But that's the point, Dorothy. Most people can't communi-cate with spirits. Take me, for example. I can't hear a thing from them."

This was an opportunity I had long waited for.

"You might not be able to speak to them, but I suspect you can feel them."

Em glanced away, just briefly, but it was enough for me to know she wished she could retract her words. When she met my eyes again, her voice was as implacable as ever.

"Don't you think if I had any ability like that, I would have said something?"

I was certain she lied, but couldn't figure out why she would bother. What was the point in denying she could sometimes sense Bec and the gang? It wasn't as if I wouldn't believe her.

"I must be mistaken." I tried to keep my voice easy, although knowing she lied made me uncomfortable. What was she hiding? "So, David Evans. What should I do about him?"

"Once the tour plans are more definite, I'll get in touch with him and schedule a meeting. He's in LA, so you won't be going out of your way."

"Okay, make a time with him, although I can't imagine what he wants."

She made a note in the diary. "We'll find out soon enough, won't we?"

Em's plans for a North American tour were progressing. After much debate, we had decided Em would handle the arrangements herself rather than engaging an agent. She had looked into several who had offered their services, and although we had conducted video interviews we hadn't been able to agree on one. Her preference was a small, slimy man called Mark Smithers, who licked his lips before he spoke and gave me the creeps. Em thought he was well-qualified and had good contacts.

My preference was a straight-talking, no-nonsense woman called Amelia Margerite but Em thought she didn't have enough experience to handle a tour of the magnitude we planned. So Em managed the negotiations herself and I suspected she was happier about that, anyway. She was planning an eight-week tour starting in New York and finishing in LA. Dates were filling up fast, both for TV appearances and for one-on-one consultations.

When she first started talking about a tour, I had thought she meant for me to do appearances in the style of David Evans: a conference room packed with people waiting for the chance to be randomly selected to connect with their dearly departed. I was uncomfortable with being treated like a performing monkey, but apparently that wasn't what she was planning at all. To my surprise, Em thought I should continue with my usual one-on-one consultations to maintain privacy for my clients. In fact, she was reserving a couple of days a week for individual consultations.

She did, however, want me to increase my fees. Given that I was booked out for months ahead, she argued that there was sufficient demand to justify a price rise. I had vetoed that, at least for now. Being able to make contact with a lost loved one shouldn't be available only to the wealthy. I charged a hundred and fifty dollars, which wasn't cheap, but was at least in the realm of what someone could save up for. Em thought I could double that without affecting bookings, but I stood firm.

I had more than enough money to be certain I would never lose my house. After this tour, I would be able to pay off my mortgage and I wouldn't ever need to work again. I would continue offering consultations, though. My clients needed me. I brought them peace and comfort. I wasn't doing it for the money anymore and I never wanted to lose sight of that.

THIRTY-SIX

I was so busy that I barely had time to think about the upcoming tour. Then suddenly June arrived and with it, winter, or at least what passed for winter in Brisbane. On the first Thursday in June, I found myself in a taxi and on my way to meet Em at the airport. This time, it was Em who slept most of the way and me who passed the flight staring out the window or watching movies. She woke a couple of hours before we were due to land and we passed the time chatting easily. I was relieved she wasn't acting oddly as she had on our last trip.

We started on the east side of the country this time and would make our way across to Los Angeles, stopping for a couple of days in major cities along the way. Em had kept our first day in New York free and I was grateful for the opportunity to walk outside in the sun and try to adjust to the time zone. I spent the rest of the day by the hotel pool, relishing having left winter behind.

The busyness I remembered from my last US trip began the next morning with a four a.m. start for a live TV breakfast show. Em had scheduled a full day of back-to-back interviews with the last finishing at eight p.m. I was too exhausted to eat by then and it was all I could do to stumble up to my room on the fourteenth floor. I felt Gray arrive and muttered a greeting before falling into the deep sleep of exhaustion.

My one-on-one consultations began the following day. Em had hired a small interview room in the hotel and allocated each client exactly thirty minutes. Since I had stood firm on not increasing my fee, Em had proposed allowing only twenty minutes per person instead of my usual hour. I vetoed that too, so she consoled herself by rigidly applying the thirty-minute timeframe we finally agreed on. She would warn me with a quiet "five minutes" as we neared the end of each appointment and waited by the door at the thirty-minute mark to escort out the client and usher in the next.

The pace was exhausting. At home, I was accustomed to an hour per client with a half hour break between. I discovered now that Em had packed the consultations in like sardines with four thirty-minute appointments before a fifteen-minute break. Lunch was one hour. Between nine a.m. and sixty-thirty p.m., I would see sixteen clients. I had consultations three days a week and media interviews for three days. The interviews were where the real money was, though. One particular interview in LA would bring in almost a quarter of a million dollars.

Sundays were my day off, although Em had warned I would need to be prepared to accept the occasional additional interview as word-of-mouth grew. Her initial plan had been to leave one or two spare spots in each interview day, which she could fill as needed. She hadn't mentioned changing her mind, but I now discovered that she had filled every interview slot. Sunday was indeed the only time I could fit in anything else, although I resolved to insist on taking at least half the day off. I was so exhausted by the end of the first day that I wondered whether I would make it through the rest of the week, let alone the whole eight week tour.

Gray was, as always, invaluable. As the only spirit who could leave the house, he was my sole contact during the tour. As the days passed and we moved from city to city, the strain showed in his voice. I worried I was pushing him too hard, but he never complained. I wondered sometimes why he did it. Just because he was somehow connected to me didn't mean he had to oblige my constant requests for communication with various spirits.

My clients were no different from those at home. They wanted contact with lost spouses, parents, siblings, dear friends. Some wanted to apologise. Many just cried and listened to what the spirit had to say. I had surprisingly few unpleasant experiences like the murdered lightbulb-shattering Michael. I hadn't encountered any others who seemed able to impact on the physical world, or at least not that they showed in my consultations. Even my unease at Bec and Lissa's abilities had diminished. Nobody had tipped me out of a chair or moved my salad items in weeks, and Lissa hadn't taken possession of any more knives. I didn't know whether they couldn't do those things anymore or if they just restrained themselves when I was around. I didn't want to ask. In truth, I didn't want to know.

I took comfort in the familiarity of my routine. I no longer waited with bated breath every time I asked for contact. Gray never let me down, not once. He was my island in a whirling maelstrom of madness during this tour. Until the day he wasn't.

THIRTY-SEVEN

By the end of June, we were in Los Angeles. We would spend a week here before heading up to Washington and then Canada before returning to LA for the flight home.

My first LA client was Jane Smith. That was the name she gave, anyway. To me, she didn't look like a Jane. I expected her to be blonde and petite, but she was a large woman. Not fat, just tall and solid. Big-boned, my mother would have called her. Her hair was almost completely grey, although she didn't look much older than her mid-forties. She was clearly nervous when Em showed her into the small room in which we were holding my consultations. I noticed Em give her hand a reassuring squeeze, which somewhat surprised me. She was always so careful to offer my clients nothing but professionalism. She didn't usually add any personal touches.

Jane perched on the edge of the chair and refused Em's offer of coffee or water. Her gaze darted around the room as if she looked for evidence of the spirits.

"How can I help you today, Ms Smith?" I made a show of making myself comfortable in my chair.

Usually my clients would relax if they thought I was at ease, but it didn't work with Jane Smith. One hand clutched her handbag, her fingernails digging into the unfortunate handle, while the other held the arm of the chair as if she thought it was about to be ripped out from beneath her. She didn't answer but continued to look around the room. I wondered whether she was on drugs. She was acting very peculiarly.

"Ms Smith? Are you all right?"

She finally looked at me.

"Ms Smith?"

She shook her head, as if trying to shake away an unwelcome thought.

"Sorry. Bit distracted at the moment," she said.

"Is there someone you would like me to contact for you?"

She studied me for a long moment.

"I'm sorry," she said finally.

"It's not a problem. Let's get started, shall we? Who would you like to contact?"

She looked down at her lap. Both hands clutched her handbag now, squeezing it as if it was a living creature and she wanted to throttle the life out of it.

"I'm really very sorry," she said to the handbag. "But I don't know what else to do. I can't go on like this."

I waited in silence. I didn't know how to reply.

Gray spoke then, his voice oddly strained.

"Dorothy, there's something strange about her. I can see... something. I don't know what it is."

"He only goes to people who can hear him." Ms Smith's eyes were desperate, haunted, with shadows beneath them. "That's why he came to me. I can hear, you see. I've never found anyone else, but she says you can. Everyone says you can."

A tendril of icy fear wrapped itself around my bowels. I had no idea what she meant, but the desperation in her face and the flatness in her voice chilled me.

"Dorothy, get rid of her," Gray said. "Now. Get her out of here."

"Ms Smith," I started. "Perhaps—"

"It's too late." Her eyes shone. "He already knows. He heard the spirit, just like I did. I know he told you to get me out of here."

I was frozen with fear.

"He goes from one of us to another," she said. "He finds someone who can hear him and he stays with them until he finds the next. I've spent eight years searching for someone else who could hear the spirits. You're the first I've found. And I'm sorry, but you'll be the next one he goes to."

"Dorothy, get her out now," Gray said.

"I think you should leave." I went to the door and opened it for her. "Please. I don't know what's wrong, but you need to go."

"It's too late." Tears trickled down her cheeks, but she looked relieved rather than sorrowful. "He's already left me. You'll feel him soon. The only way to get rid of him is to find someone else who can hear him."

As she spoke, I felt a hand rest lightly against the small of my back. Icy fingers tapped their way up my spine. Then something settled around my shoulders, around my neck. It was light and insubstantial, but there was definitely something there. I put my hand to my throat but felt nothing. Not with my fingers, at any rate.

"You feel him, don't you?" She smiled now, although she didn't look happy. "I am so, so sorry. I swore I'd never do this to someone else. When it happened to me, I vowed I'd keep him until I died. I thought that if he was still attached to me then, it might drag him out of this world.

But I can't cope with it anymore. I have to pass him on. I'm so sorry."

She fled.

I ran my fingers over my neck but felt nothing other than my skin, warm to my touch. There was something there, though. I could feel it against my skin, so why couldn't I touch it? My fingers felt the way my pulse leaped, but they couldn't feel the thing around my neck.

I tried to steady my breath. Tried to tell myself it was nothing. I was just freaked out, that's all. It was because of her odd behaviour. The feeling of something wrapped around my neck would pass once I calmed down.

The door opened and Em entered. Her gaze went straight to my neck.

"You can see it," I whispered. "What is it?"

She shook her head, eyes wide. "It went to you."

"What do you mean?"

"I- I saw it when she came in. I..."

Her voice trailed away and she briefly put her hands over her face.

"I don't know what to say," she said, at last.

"I think she was trying to tell me she was being haunted and somehow she's passed it to me. What does it look like?"

"It's dark. Insubstantial. Like a storm cloud around your neck. How does it feel?"

"Uncomfortable. It's not constricting my throat, but it feels like it could if it wanted to."

Em took a couple of deep breaths, as if trying to compose herself.

"We need to move on with the consultations," she said. "You're close to running late."

"Gray, do you know what this thing is?" I asked.

He didn't respond.

"Gray?"

Still no reply.

Em gave me an odd look. "Are you ready to go on?"

"No, I need to talk to Gray."

"Who?"

"My... one of..." Of course, I had never told her about how my ability worked. It was one of Bec's rules: they wanted to remain anonymous and I was supposed to let people think I had some kind of magical ability. And Em had never asked. "One of my spirit friends. He's not answering me."

"Can't you deal with that later? You have clients waiting."

"You don't understand. I don't speak directly to the spirits my clients want. My friends, my spirit contacts, liaise with them for me."

"So use another contact. Dorothy, we need to move on."

"I can't use another contact. Gray is the only one who can travel outside of the house."

She seemed to blanch a little, but quickly recovered her usual professional facade.

"How long is it going to take you to restore contact? I can tell the clients that you need to rest a little. Move a few things around. You'll have to go a bit later tonight, though, to get through all your consultations." She scrolled through a list on her tablet. "I can give you maybe forty minutes. You'll be running half an hour late by that point. That's a whole consultation. The next client—"

"The next client will just have to wait," I snapped. "Can't you see I have a problem? Without Gray, I can't communicate with the spirits."

She looked up at me, although her gaze lingered on the thing around my neck.

"So, how do you contact him?" she asked.

"He's always just there when I call for him. He has never not answered me before."

"And you're sure you can't contact any of your other... contacts?"

"Not from here. I can only speak to them when I'm in the house."

Her gaze returned to my neck. "Do you think that, um..."

I waited.

"Maybe the, um, that thing is blocking your contact?"

Panic welled within me and I tried to push it down.

"Gray?" I said. "Gray, please, if you can hear me but you can't speak for some reason, can you give me a sign?"

Nothing. But of course, I shouldn't expect a sign from him. Unlike Bec and Lissa, he had never had any ability to impact on the physical world.

"How do I get rid of it?" I asked.

Em's eyes were wide as she shook her head. I had never seen her lose her professional composure before, but she looked like she was fighting the urge to flee.

"She said it would go to whoever can hear it," I said. "She said she'd had it for eight years." Goosebumps spread over my body as I understood what Ms Smith had been trying to tell me. "This thing attached itself to her eight years ago and it's taken her that long to find someone else who can hear the spirits."

"Has it said anything?" Em asked. "She— that is, I wonder if it can speak?"

"No."

Perhaps if it would speak to me, I could try to reason with it, convince it to leave. But wouldn't Jane Smith have tried that? Wouldn't, if it was open to argument, she have found the right words in the eight years she had spent with it?

"I'm stuck with it, aren't I? Until I find someone else."

"There will be a way," Em said. "We can look into exorcisms

and banishments. I'll see what I can find out about getting rid of malignant spirits. In the meantime, I'd suggest you try not to upset it. We need to move on."

"What do you want me to do? I can't do anything without Gray."

"Dorothy, listen to me." Em spoke calmly as if to a distraught child. "We have to move on. Is there any way you can call on another spirit?"

I shook my head. Em's mouth twitched and I knew she could see her oh-so-carefully planned schedule lying in tatters.

"So what do we do?" she asked. "What about your clients? There are three waiting for you out there and more due to arrive soon. One of them has driven six hours to get here."

"There's nothing I can do."

I felt wretched at letting my clients down, but what choice did I have? This was utterly beyond my control. The disappointed clients would get over it. I was more worried about what had happened to Gray.

"Gray, are you there?"

I knew he wasn't. I couldn't feel him at all, but I had to try again. Perhaps he would hear me and come back. Please let him be all right. Was it possible for a spirit to die a second time?

"What am I supposed to do with the people waiting out there?" Em asked. "We can't leave them sitting around all day while you try to connect with your contact. We've got to move on."

"What do you want me to do, Em? Don't you understand? Gray's gone. I don't know what's happened, but I can't contact him. I can't help the clients who are waiting. Until I can reach Gray again, I can't do anything."

"You'll have to fake it until he comes back. We have too much riding on this tour to cancel consultations just because your spirit won't talk to you. We have to keep to the schedule."

"Screw the schedule. I can't lie to those people. Give them their money back. I can't do anything without Gray."

"You can't cancel, Dorothy. Every cent you make depends on people believing in you. If you cancel just because your spirit has decided to go off somewhere else for a while, you'll get a reputation for being flaky. That's something you can't afford in this business. Just fake it until Gray comes back. That's what all the other speakers do. Those people out there don't care what you say, anyway. They just want someone to tell them their dearly departed is in a better place and still loves them."

"Can you hear yourself, Em? You want me to lie, just like everyone else? These people come to me because I've got a reputation for being legitimate. 'The real thing', remember? I can't lie to them. I'll go out and speak to them, tell them I can't contact the spirits at the moment. They'll understand. I'm sure they'd rather my honesty than that I take their money and lie to them."

"It's not lying to them. It's giving them reassurance. Peace of mind. They're sitting out there waiting, Dorothy. Waiting for you. One of them has been here since five a.m. She was worried she'd get stuck in traffic and miss her appointment, so she arrived five hours early. You can't let them down. You have to at least try. Maybe Gray will come back in a few minutes. In the meantime, you need to move on. Give these people what they came here for."

"But I can't give them what they came for. I'd be lying to them."

"What about the, uh, thing?" She gestured towards my neck. "Can it do anything to help?"

The spirit, or whatever it was, was still and silent.

"I don't know if I can communicate with it and even if I could, I wouldn't know whether to trust it."

"Then we have no other options." Her voice was all business. "You'll just have to fake it until the spirits decide to speak to you again."

How could I let my clients down? What about that poor woman who drove six hours? And the one who arrived five hours early? Em could keep track of who got cheated and next time I came here, I'd find them all and do another consultation for free, make sure they got what they paid for. That made me feel better. I took a deep breath. I was about to do the worst thing I had ever done in my life.

"Okay, let's move on."

My voice sounded calm, but inside I felt like a puddle of half-set pudding.

Em bared her teeth and I wasn't sure whether it was meant to be a smile or a grimace.

"I'll bring in the next client."

CHAPTER

THIRTY-EIGHT

The next client's name was Jemima and she looked even less like her name than Jane Smith did. She was at least a hundred kilos of muscle topped with a spiky crew cut threaded with blue streaks. She had a strong jaw and a no-nonsense air about her. I was already feeling intimidated, even before I realised there was a problem, and it wasn't just that I couldn't speak with Gray.

Jemima requested contact with Peter Withers, aged thirty-four. An ugly bastard, she said, and my stomach sank. This would be an uncomfortable session. Hopefully, not a repeat of the lightbulb-shattering incident, though. If it was another angry spirit, how much worse might the situation be if I couldn't hear what he wanted me to pass on?

"Speak to me, spirits. I'm seeking Peter Withers, aged thirty-four."

I kept my eyes closed as I always did while I waited for Gray to connect with the requested spirit. At least it meant I didn't have to make eye contact with the client while I waited.

Jemima shifted in her chair and it squeaked in protest. I'd squeak too if she sat on me. I waited another breath or two for good measure. She might get suspicious if I was too fast. Jemima shifted again.

"Does it usually take this long?" Her voice was aggressive and I tried not to flinch.

"Not usually. My spirit contacts must be having trouble finding him."

"He'd be hard to miss. Big, ugly, mean bloke. You tell 'em that and they'll find him no problems."

"They usually don't need anything other than a name and age. Anyway, sorry to keep you waiting." I forced as much confidence into my voice as I could and prayed she would believe me. "I've made contact with Peter now."

I paused, hoping she would volunteer some information. I supposed this is what the fakes did. Looked for clues and made it up as they went.

"So what does the ugly son of a bitch have to say for himself?"

I hoped she didn't see me gulp.

"He asks how you are," I said cautiously, hoping her response would lead me in the right direction.

She barked a short laugh.

"Are you kidding? How do you think I am, you bastard? You knock me up, beat me half to death, and then have the nerve to go and die on me. I'm peachy, just peachy."

I clenched my hands together in my lap, hoping she wouldn't see the way they trembled. This could get ugly if I got anything wrong.

"He says he didn't exactly intend to die." I figured this was a safe guess.

Jemima hissed, a long intake of breath through clenched teeth.

"Then why did the lousy bastard shoot himself in the head? Seems to me like he intended to die. Son of a bitch. Were you trying to screw up the rest of my life? How did you think I was going to bring up a baby on my own, huh? How did you think I was going to pay for a baby?"

I thought quickly. "He didn't really intend to shoot himself. He just wanted to give you a fright."

"Why the hell would he want to do that?"

Was it my imagination or had her voice softened?

"He says you'd been fighting a lot. He wanted you to remember how much you loved him."

"Son of a bitch."

I had no idea what else to say. I had to get rid of her before I exposed myself.

"I'm losing contact with Peter. Is there anything else you want to say to him?"

"I miss you, you ugly bastard," she said. Obviously not a woman prone to moments of tenderness. "And I'll never forgive you for leaving me."

"He's gone now."

I opened my eyes in time to catch her wiping away a tear. Perhaps she was prone to some tenderness after all.

I've never forgiven myself for what I did to my clients that day. I should have been upfront and told them the truth. Or at least said I had to cancel because I was sick. Instead, I faked it. I took careful note of their clothes, their faces, the clues they dropped in conversation, and I made it all up.

"Well, that wasn't so bad, was it?" Em asked brightly after the last client left. "No complaints and they all seemed satisfied, even Penny, the one who drove six hours to get here. She gave me a hug and thanked me as she left."

I departed without a word. I had done something awful today and she was gloating about it. Normally we would walk to the elevator together and she would tell me about our dinner plans. Today she just watched me leave.

I examined myself in the elevator's mirrored wall. I could feel the thing around my neck, but couldn't see any sign of it. Not even a shadow against my skin. The elevator doors opened and I made my way down the hallway to my room. I let myself in and closed the door behind me.

"Gray?" I asked.

Perhaps it had been a momentary glitch. A loss of signal, so to speak. Too much noise down there. But Gray didn't respond.

I went to the bathroom, although I already knew the mirror wouldn't show the thing around my neck. As I expected, I saw nothing other than my own image, my face flushed, my hair flying in all directions, but still just me. I stared hard at my neck. As if it knew I looked for it, the spirit squeezed my throat. Not hard, just a reminder.

"I know you're there," I said. "I can feel you. What do you want?"

Silence. I supposed it was too much to expect I might be able to communicate with it. Perhaps a shower would calm me down. If I could just think more clearly, I might figure out a solution. I turned away from the mirror and started to undress.

There was a sound like static, then a soft hissing.

"You."

I froze, my shirt half off. I tugged it back on.

"Can you hear me?" I asked.

Again, there was a delay before it answered.

"Yesss."

"What do you want?" Surely it could feel the way my heart pounded.

"You."

"Why me?"

"You. Can hear."

"Yes, I can hear you. Tell me what you want."

"You."

"But why me?"

"Can hear."

I tried a different tactic. "What do you want to say?"

"Can hear me."

I asked a couple more times, but it didn't respond again. Maybe it had gone to sleep, or maybe it had said everything it had to say.

"I'm going to have a shower now," I said. "Could you maybe close your eyes or something?"

There was no response. I've never felt more vulnerable than the first time I undressed in front of that thing. I told myself it couldn't see me, but I was wrong.

"Nicccce," it hissed once I was naked.

My instinct was to grab a towel and wrap it around myself and never again undress until I had got rid of it. Instead, I took a deep breath and turned on the shower.

Eight years. She coped for eight years, but she probably didn't have the spirit friends that I did. I'd be able to talk to them again once I got home. We were a long way apart, after all. Once I was home and could speak with my friends, we'd find a way to get rid of it. It might take a couple of weeks, but then it would be gone.

CHAPTER
THIRTY-NINE

My sleep that night was restless and never for more than a few minutes. I kept waking with a start, gasping for breath, thinking the thing around my neck was strangling me in my sleep. I couldn't think of it as a spirit. This thing was nothing like bossy Bec, ditzy Lissa, silent Samson, and stoic Gray. If I didn't call it a spirit, what else was there? Devil? Demon?

The thing, whatever it was, didn't speak again. Each time I woke, breathless and panting, it would gently squeeze my neck. I could have almost thought of that as a hello if it weren't for the vibes of wrongness coming off the demon.

The night dragged on as I tossed and turned. It normally didn't bother me, being on my own at night. It was nice to have the bed to myself. Nobody else taking up space or snoring or pulling away the covers. I had been single for a long time and thought I was past worrying about that. I had buried myself in my work and told myself I wasn't lonely. But tonight it would have been nice to have someone here with me. Someone to put their arms around me and tell me it would be okay, that we'd find a way to get rid of the demon, that together we'd solve the problem.

By morning I was exhausted. The demon gave me a gentle squeeze, as if letting me know it too had woken. I dragged myself out of bed and hit the shower, avoiding the mirror. Looking at it wouldn't change anything. Whether I looked or not, the thing was still there.

When I went down to the restaurant, Em was at a corner booth, nursing a very large coffee. A fat ring-binder sat beside her on the table. I slid into the booth and took a grateful sip from the coffee that waited for me.

"Thanks," I said.

I glanced up to see Em staring at my neck.

"It's still there," she said.

I nodded. There was nothing else to say.

"I had hoped..." Her voice trailed away.

"I know. Me too."

We sipped our coffee in silence for a few moments.

"I did some research." Em pushed the ring-binder across the table to me.

I opened the binder and flicked through pages of internet prints and handwritten notes.

"You must have been up all night," I said.

If I hadn't glanced up just then, I would have missed the look on her face.

"Em, what is it? I feel like there's something you're not telling me."

She shook her head and gulped down the rest of her coffee.

"I'm just tired. It's been a long week. Anyway, read the stuff in the folder. I've highlighted passages that look the most promising. You've got exactly thirty minutes for breakfast and then I need you in the consultation room."

I sighed.

"Em, I can't. I can't just lie to people."

"There is no other option. But it's the last day of individual consultations for now. The rest of the week is all interviews, so you'll have a few days to try to connect with your spirits again before the next round of consultations."

"Tell them I'm sick."

"Some of these people have driven—"

"I don't want to hear it. Tell them we'll keep their details and make it up to them, but I'm not doing consultations today."

She started to argue, but I held up my hand.

"I mean it, Em. I'm not going to discuss this any further. There will be no more consultations until I can reach the spirits again."

She sat there for a moment or two longer, then got to her feet.

"I will go tell them then. They're going to be extremely disappointed."

She hesitated, as if waiting for me to change my mind. I kept my gaze on my coffee and said nothing. Finally, she walked away.

I sighed and scrubbed at my eyes, wiping away a few tears. Cancelling the consultations was better than lying to everyone and I shouldn't feel bad about it. If people knew the truth, they would much rather keep their money than have me pretending I had made contact with their loved ones.

I thumbed through the binder. Pages and pages detailing ways to exorcise a demon. My heart beat a little faster as I skimmed the headings. I could barely focus on the words. I had been thinking of the thing as a demon, but it was confronting to realise that Em had come to the same conclusion. Was I possessed?

I read highlighted passages here and there. An article about priests who performed exorcisms. Several about herbs or potions that were supposed to make a person invisible to demons. Article after article about people who claimed to have rid themselves of the demons who had possessed them. Most of these had sceptical comments in the margins in Em's handwriting, but a couple had notes indicating she had taken a particular story more seriously. Next to one article, she had written in neat capital letters: *Came uninvited, seems malignant. But came with invited guest. Does that make it invited too? Harder to remove if invited.*

I scanned the pages almost feverishly, hoping like hell the demon couldn't read. I didn't want to know how it might react if it figured out what I was doing. By the time I closed the binder and pushed it away, I was thoroughly discouraged. It seemed exorcising a demon wasn't a simple matter. There were rituals to be conducted, all involving certain phases of the moon, specific words to be said, or potions that must be drunk prior to the ritual.

I couldn't do anything like that while I was away. We were only halfway through the tour. I still had another four weeks to get through. My flight home wasn't until August twenty-fourth. How would I get through another four weeks of this?

CHAPTER

FORTY

With my consultations cancelled, I devoted the day and most of the night to trying to reach Gray, but heard nothing but silence from the other side of the veil. I read more of Em's ring binder, but looking at her many pages of meticulous research made me feel even worse. Surely if there was actually a way to rid myself of this thing she would have already found it, given how much research she had done.

By morning, I was a wreck. I had hardly slept, I was sick with worry about Gray, and I had worked myself up into such a state of panic that I could barely think. The only thing that got me out of bed was the knowledge that my meeting with David Evans was today. If he was legitimate, the demon would surely hear him. I might be rid of it in just a few hours.

I went down to the hotel restaurant for breakfast well before six. Em was already there nursing a coffee. She was immaculately dressed as usual, her bob as sleek as ever, but there were black bags under her eyes and her fingers moved restlessly over the table.

The waiter poured me a coffee, and we sipped our drinks in

silence. My stomach churned and when the waiter returned to take our orders, we both waved him away. I was determined not to speak first. It took two cups of coffee before she did.

"What are we going to do?"

"Cancel the rest of the tour, I suppose." I set my mug down and fiddled with an empty sugar packet. "I can't see any way around it."

"You still can't contact your spirit?"

"Don't you think I would have said something if I could?"

She blinked at me and I finally realised she didn't even know how mad I was that she had pressured me to lie to my clients. I opened my mouth to tell her, but thought the better of it. My business was in tatters. I wouldn't need a manager once we got home. There was no point in deliberately destroying our relationship as well.

How solid were my finances without the income from this tour? This was supposed to set me up for life. I didn't even know how much I had in the bank as Em had been looking after everything. Once I got home, I'd have to sit down and figure out how long the money would last. God knew I could do with a break before I had to make any decisions about what to do next. Em had kept me to a punishing schedule for months now and I was exhausted.

"Dorothy, you know you have to keep going, right?" Em asked.

"Keep going with what?"

"The tour, of course. You're committed to the eight weeks. You've signed contracts. Those are legally binding agreements. You can't just cancel because the spirits don't want to play ball anymore."

I gave her a bewildered look. How was it possible that she still didn't understand?

"Think of how much money all these TV channels have

already spent promoting your appearances," she said. "If you pull out, they'll probably sue."

"I can explain to them. I can call them—"

"Are you kidding? You think they'll believe you? They'll think it's an excuse, that you're scared and looking for a reason to pull out."

"Em, I am scared. I don't know what's happened to Gray. I don't know whether the others know either, but I've got to get home and find out. He's my friend and something has happened to him."

"He's probably crossed over," she said irritably. "That's what spirits are supposed to do after all."

"I'm pulling out of the tour," I said. "There is no other option."

We argued for some time and eventually she convinced me to keep going for a little longer. Give Gray time to reappear, she said. Once I'd pulled out, it would be too late to change my mind if he came back. I agreed to wait a couple of days — three or four, no more — before I made a final decision. At least I didn't have any interviews today.

If David Evans was a true speaker, would the demon automatically leave me as soon as it saw him, or did I need to do something else first? Was there a keyword or something? Jane Smith would be able to tell me. I asked Em for her phone number, but she didn't have it. She seemed somewhat bewildered by that and assured me she collected a phone number for every client. She needed to be able to contact them in case I fell ill. But without a phone number, I had no way of trying to track down Jane Smith. It probably wasn't even her real name.

Em had arranged for a car to take me to my meeting with David Evans, which was to be in his suite at the five-star hotel he lived in. He certainly wasn't slumming it, I thought, as I walked into the expansive foyer. The demon around my neck felt particularly heavy today. I wondered if it could sense my hope that I'd shortly be rid of it.

"Dorothy Marks," I said to the receptionist. "I'm meeting with David Evans."

The receptionist, a skinny little man of about twenty, wearing black pants, a white business shirt and a slim black tie, ran his finger down a list of names.

"Of course, Ms Marks." He was all smoothness and efficiency. "Mr Evans let us know he was expecting you. He's in suite five twelve. The lift is just over there behind you. When you get to the fifth floor, five twelve will be the second door on your left. I'll call and let him know you're on your way up."

"Thank you."

As I waited for the lift, I wiped my sweaty palms on my skirt. I would have been intimidated to meet David Evans anyway, but although he might not know it, these circumstances were anything but normal. In just a few moments, I'd know whether he was a genuine speaker.

I knocked on the door of five twelve. There were footsteps inside and then the door was opened by a waif of a woman, all big, dark eyes and tousled hair. She looked like she was barely into her twenties. Was she his assistant or a prostitute? I tried not to judge her tiny red skirt and see-through black blouse that clearly displayed her nipples. Her lipstick was smudged, leaving me wondering what I had interrupted.

She stared at me blankly. "Yes?"

"I'm Dorothy Marks. I have an appointment with David Evans."

She looked back over her shoulder into the room. "Dave, someone here to see you."

"That will be Dorothy." His voice was hearty and jovial. "Bring her in."

"You didn't tell me you had a meeting this morning." She glared at me as if it was my fault.

"It's on my calendar, sweetheart. Did you look?"

She didn't answer him but did at least hold the door open wider and indicate with a jerk of her head for me to enter. She didn't smile.

My heart pounded. One more minute. Less than that even. And then I might be free of the demon. The woman closed the door and stood there, glaring at me. I waited, looking around the room to avoid staring back at her.

"Well, show her in, Miranda." He sounded exasperated.

"You didn't say that before. What do you think I am, a mind reader?" She pointed to a door. "That way."

Then she walked over to a couch and flung herself into it.

I hesitated in front of the door Miranda had gestured at. Was I supposed to knock or just go in? The door opened before I could decide, and there he was.

David Evans was a big man. What might have been muscle in his youth had gone to fat. His blond hair was meticulously groomed and when he extended his hand to me, I noticed his nails were long and carefully manicured.

"Dorothy, do come in. Where has that scrag gone?" He spotted her draped over the couch. "Oi. Get up, you lazy cow, and make us some coffee."

"I'll make you something all right," she muttered as she slowly climbed out of the couch.

David wrapped an arm around my shoulders and pulled me into the room, closing the door behind us.

"Dorothy, I'm so pleased to finally meet you. I've heard so much about you. You've really been making a splash, eh?"

"It's a pleasure to meet you."

I hoped my instant dislike for him wasn't apparent in my

voice. The demon didn't seem to be making any move to go to him. Perhaps it hadn't woken up yet.

"Please, sit down."

He released my shoulders and gestured vaguely to where a pair of long leather couches positioned by floor to ceiling windows took advantage of the view of LA. The only other furniture in the room was a sideboard with a tall vase standing on either side.

I sat in the centre of one couch and, to my relief, he chose the other. I had worried he might sit right next to me. As he settled himself, I waited for any indication that the demon stirred. Perhaps these things took some time, or maybe it was asleep.

"So, Dorothy." He beamed at me, revealing shiny, impossibly white teeth. Despite his overall size, his teeth seemed too big for his mouth. I was struck by the thought that perhaps he wanted to bite me with those enormous teeth. I pushed the stupid thought away and tried to concentrate on David. He waited, still smiling, and if he thought there was anything odd in my delayed response, it didn't show in his face.

"It's nice to meet you." Had I already said that? Why hadn't the demon noticed him?

His shiny smile grew even wider.

"How are you, Dorothy? Always such a buzz to meet a fellow spiritualist. Not many of us around, are there? And so nice to see a young one on the up-and-up. Gives me a real thrill. And now to finally meet you. You just let me know if there's any way I can help you out, eh? Always happy to share my experience with a newbie. I could mentor you or whatever, eh?"

He kept talking and I tried to keep an interested look on my face while marvelling that someone could take so long and use so many words to say absolutely nothing. I held my breath, trying to keep myself absolutely still so I could feel whether the demon moved at all. If David noticed I wasn't listening, it didn't stop his patter. We must have passed fifteen minutes in that way before he finally remembered Miranda. He stood and cracked open the door.

"Oi, where's the coffee, you lazy scrag?"

She returned fire with a comment I couldn't quite hear, but he stepped into the other room for a moment and closed the door behind him. There was a brief argument before he returned.

"Don't know why I put up with that lazy cow," he said. "I should have fired her months ago."

"Why don't you?"

"Little tart serves me well in a number of ways," he said with a wink. "If you get my meaning."

At least that answered the question of whether she was his assistant or his whore.

Miranda stomped in with a tray bearing a coffee pot and assorted items. She dumped it on the sideboard, ignoring the liquid that sloshed from the pot, and stomped away. David poured me a coffee, splashed in milk and a cube of sugar without asking what I wanted, and then continue his spiel as he served his own coffee.

I sipped my drink, wondering how long I would have to stay before I could a) be absolutely certain the demon wasn't going to transfer to David, and b) get the hell out of here. He continued to talk about absolutely nothing and didn't seem to notice that I never replied. I finished my coffee and went to get up to take my mug to the sideboard, but the demon stirred, tightening its grip on my neck. I sat back very slowly, not wanting to distract it if it had sensed David.

I crossed my legs and tried to look casual as I raised one hand to my neck. The demon moved slightly, repositioning itself. I held my breath and prayed it was preparing to leave.

Then it settled again and seemed to go back to sleep or whatever it did when it didn't move.

David's chatter washed over me as I tried to keep the disappointment from showing on my face. Tears welled and I blinked quickly as I willed them away. I had really thought this might be a chance to get rid of the demon, but it clearly wasn't going anywhere. That meant David was a fake. If he had been a true speaker, I would have been rid of this curse around my neck and I wouldn't have even felt guilty about passing it onto him since he was so unlikeable. He finally stopped for breath and I jumped in without thinking.

"So David, how do you do it?"

He gave me a polished smile and seemed to pretend he didn't know what I meant.

"What techniques do you use? You know, do you look for wedding rings, a locket around the neck, prematurely grey hair?"

I wanted to be certain before I left. I didn't want to wonder later whether I had simply not given the demon enough time. David opened his mouth, the look on his face indicating he was about to protest, but I forestalled him with a wink and a tap on the side of my nose.

"Come on, you can share some trade secrets with me. After all, you and I both know the truth, don't we?"

He wouldn't be suspicious. He was too full of himself to think I might be doing anything other than trying to pry trade secrets out of him. Sure enough, he grinned, once again exposing his over-sized teeth. I tried not to shudder.

"Dorothy, you're a naughty little minx, aren't you?"

I raised my eyebrows at him and tried to look like I was smirking. It probably wasn't terribly convincing, but it was enough.

"It's all of that and so, so much more," he said. "You need to be an expert reader of body language. You need to interpret the way someone dresses, the mannerisms they use. I look at what sort of handbag they have, what kind of jewellery they wear, whether their nails are manicured. It all helps. It all adds up to a more complete picture of the person you're dealing with, giving you that little bit more ammunition to pack your guns with, so to speak."

I disliked him. Intensely. It was a pity I couldn't contact Gray because I would have loved to pass on a message from a spirit connected to David. I wanted to show him I wasn't like him. I wasn't just another fraud.

He continued to talk. I stopped listening and focussed instead on the demon, willing it to notice him. It never stirred. David kept talking when I got up to put the mug on the sideboard. I waited there for a few moments, but he was far too absorbed in his own words.

"Well, I need to be off now," I said, interrupting his flow.

He looked surprised to see me standing there.

"Oh, don't leave yet, Dot," he said. "You only just got here."

"Yes, well, very busy, I'm afraid," I said.

I went to the door but paused with my hand on the knob. This was exactly when I needed Gray to pop back into my life and offer me some choice gossip, just like he had when Mac fired me. But Gray didn't speak and the demon still didn't move.

"Goodbye then," I said and left.

Miranda lay sprawled on the couch, too busy examining her nails to look at me. I held my head high as I left the suite. In the hallway, I held my finger on the button for the lift and prayed it would arrive before I burst into tears.

FORTY-ONE

I spent another sleepless night trying to contact Gray. I even tried to talk to the demon, but if it heard me, it never responded. What did it want? If it would just tell me, maybe I could find a way to satisfy it so that it would leave. I also spent a lot of time sobbing, with my face pressed into my pillow so Em wouldn't hear me from the room next door. If only I knew whether something had happened to Gray, or to all of my spirit friends, or if it was just the demon blocking my ability to contact him.

Sunday's interviews went smoothly enough and I was pleased to be busy because it meant I didn't have time to dwell on tomorrow's interview: Rick Firman. Last time Rick interviewed me, he sprang a surprise consultation on me and I was terrified he would do the same again. I couldn't risk having to fake my way through something like that.

"I'll see the executive producer when we arrive," Em said, as we were driven to the MoMoTV studio on Monday morning. "I'll tell them there are to be no surprises this time. That to maintain the exclusivity of your one-on-ones, you no longer do public consultations."

We arrived at MoMoTV a little late, thanks to the god-awful traffic, and the executive assistant rushed me into hair and makeup. Em caught me just before I went on stage.

"It won't happen," she assured me. "It'll be a bunch of questions, just a regular interview. Nothing to worry about."

So I felt relatively confident as I strode out onto the stage to be greeted with a handshake from Rick. The interview, as Em said, was full of the standard questions. How did I do it? Was I personally affected by my client's stories? Were there ever times when I connected with the wrong spirit? The stock questions every interviewer asked. I had my answers down pat.

"Dorothy, we've only got a few minutes left," Rick said. "And I have a very special favour to ask you. We have somebody here in the audience today who recently lost her brother."

My heart started palpitating and my palms were already sweating. Em had promised this wouldn't happen.

"She's hoping you might be able to contact him."

I stared at him, my face probably telegraphing my horror. Rick looked smug.

"Looks like Dorothy's feeling a little shy today, folks," he said to the audience. "Why don't we encourage her? Let's give her a big hand."

The audience clapped and cheered. I covered the microphone pinned to my shirt and used the noise of the audience as cover to speak to Rick.

"Didn't you get the message?"

"Sorry, Dorothy, but we'd already arranged this. It was too late by the time your manager mentioned it. That sort of thing needs to be established when you sign the contract, not five minutes before we go on air."

"I- I can't. I'm sorry, but there's no way..."

He turned back to the audience. "Come on, folks, keep it up. Dorothy needs your encouragement."

The clapping continued while he stared at me. There was no way he would give up, not with the entire audience backing him. I would have to do it. I glared at him even as I nodded my acceptance. He smirked back.

"Dorothy, please meet my special guest," he said as the noise from the audience finally died down. "This is Brenda."

The studio lights focused in on a woman in the audience. I could see little more than shadow behind the bright stage lights.

"Brenda, what's your brother's name?" Rick asked.

"Jake," she said. "Jake Miles."

Rick nodded at me. "Take it away, Dorothy."

I swallowed, my mouth dry, and took a deep breath. Just a few minutes. That's all I had to get through. A few minutes and this would be over.

"How old was Jake when he died?" I tried to sound confident, but knew I didn't pull it off. I cleared my throat.

"Twenty-seven." Her voice was cool. "He died four months ago."

I closed my eyes and took a deep breath. Anyone who had seen my last Rick Firman interview would know this was my standard practice and at least it gave me a moment to pull myself together.

"Speak to me, spirits. I'm seeking Jake Miles, aged twenty-seven." To my relief, my voice sounded stronger this time.

I waited another minute or two, feeling like centuries passed in the meantime and praying desperately that this would be the moment my connection with Gray was restored. I breathed in and out, trying to keep my breaths slow and measured. The leather seat on which I sat felt sticky and I hoped I wouldn't leave a sweaty smear when I stood up. The audience was as quiet as a studio audience ever was while they waited. I counted ten breaths in and out.

"I think I've made contact with Jake." I've always envied that professional voice Em puts on and I strove to mimic it now. "He says you look better than he expected."

Muffled laughter from the audience. Brenda said nothing. She was going to make me work for this. Normally that wouldn't bother me, but today, without Gray's assistance, it would have helped if she'd give me just a little information. Anything at all would help.

"He asks whether you're looking after yourself," I said.

"He always did like to fuss," Brenda replied.

I restrained my sigh of relief, not wanting anyone to notice. Here was something I could work with.

"He says you're his sister. He's supposed to look out for you."

"Pity he had to go get himself killed then, isn't it?" she said.

I hoped this wasn't about to become an ugly spat. Please let this not be a repeat of the lightbulb incident, not while I was being filmed in front of an audience.

"He doesn't remember how he died. That's not unusual."

"I can tell him how he died," she said.

"No, better not," I said quickly, hoping I could head off any nastiness. "If he hasn't retained that memory, there's a reason for it."

"Is there something you'd like to say to Jake, Brenda?" Rick asked.

"I'd just like to know he's all right." Brenda's voice was a little tearful now. "He's... he's my only brother and I—"

The audience sighed in sympathy.

"He's fine." If I could give her a little peace, I wouldn't feel so bad about what I was doing. "He says it's not such a bad place. He's not alone, although he still misses you. He asks if you remember the last Christmas you spent together?"

She made a noise that I took for agreement.

"He's laughing. I assume there's a private joke, but he's not telling me what. Brenda, I'm losing contact, so I'll have to talk fast. He loves you and misses you. The two of you didn't always get along, but you were the best sister he could have asked for. He says to look after yourself and that he'll be watching over you for as long as he's there on the other side of the veil."

I took a deep breath, hoping that everything I had said was generic enough to apply to any sister.

"I'm sorry, Brenda. He's gone now."

I shot a glance at Rick to find he watched me with an odd expression. He cleared his throat and I got the distinct impression he felt uncomfortable.

"Well Dorothy, that was... comprehensive," he said. I had no idea what that was supposed to mean. "Brenda, do you have any comments for Dorothy?"

"Thank you, Dorothy. That was interesting."

Interesting? My heart pounded. I got something wrong. I had tried to keep my comments vague, but something I said had told her I wasn't speaking to her dead brother. My hands trembled and I clasped them so nobody would see.

"The only problem, Dorothy," she continued, "is that I don't have a dead brother called Jake. As a matter of fact, I don't have any brothers, dead or alive."

My gaze shot from her to Rick. That explained the odd look. They had set me up. Played me. Exposed me as a fake.

I couldn't catch my breath. My heart pounded so hard it almost drowned out the noise of the audience. Almost. There were a few laughs and some hisses. The occasional jeer. I stared at Rick, unable to think of a single thing to say. He looked surprised and even a little sorry for me. That was one thing I didn't want: pity. I had got myself into a mess, but I didn't want anyone's pity. I stood and ripped the little microphone off my shirt.

"This interview is over," I hissed down at him.

"Dorothy—" he said.

I stalked off the stage. I wanted to get away. Far away. I couldn't sit there and listen to them laugh and boo. Em was waiting when I exited the stage. Her face was thunderous.

"We're leaving," she said, thrusting my handbag at me.

She marched down the hallway and I followed. Em would take care of everything. She would sort it all out. A pantsuited woman hurried towards us.

"Em." She extended her hand and arranged her face into a conciliatory expression. "Let's talk before you leave."

Em pushed straight past as if she wasn't there.

"Oh, we'll be talking all right. That is, you'll be talking to Dorothy's lawyers."

I didn't know I had a lawyer, let alone plurals of them.

The woman turned to me, but I put my head down and scurried after Em. She let us leave without any further attempt at pacification. I guess she didn't want to have that conversation any more than I did. Em hesitated as we reached the parking lot. Since we were early, our car wasn't waiting by the door as it usually would be. Then an engine started somewhere to our left and within moments the car was in front of us.

Em's face was pale and she looked like she was grinding her teeth. It was unusual for her to display so much emotion, but I was too busy having my own meltdown to think much of it. The first few blocks passed in silence. I stared at my hands in my lap, noticing that I needed to file my nails. There hadn't been time for details like that lately. I picked at a stray thread on my skirt. I should cut that off when I got back to the hotel or I'd forget until the next time I wore it.

When Em spoke, she sounded like she talked through gritted teeth.

"I can't believe they did that."

I took a deep breath, held it, released it. I was calmer now that I was away from the stage and the people staring at me.

"I don't think that's what they expected. I took them by surprise last time and showed I really could communicate with the spirits. They probably expected me to say I couldn't find her brother. Then they'd confess that he didn't exist and we'd all laugh about it."

"They set you up."

I darted a glance at her, but she stared out the window. Palm trees flashed by.

"I don't—"

"Dorothy, they set you up."

"I guess so."

"They've ruined your career."

"It was already ruined," I said. "I don't have a career if I can't contact the spirits."

"They must have known they'd ruin your career if it went wrong."

"I hardly think that was their intention."

Em finally looked at me. Her eyes were dark circles in a pale face.

"Don't you get it, Dorothy? They've ruined it. They've ruined everything."

I felt like we were talking about different things.

"Em, are you all right?"

She turned back to the window.

"They've ruined it," she said, more softly this time.

We passed the rest of the drive in silence. I wasn't sure why Em was so agitated. After all, it was my career, not hers, in tatters. Sure, she would be out of a job once we got home, but she'd have no problems getting another one. I'd write her a good reference and someone with Em's skills would walk into another position. Perhaps I could even give her a bit of a payout.

As soon as I figured out my own finances, I'd see what I could do for her.

The car pulled up at our hotel and Em climbed out in silence. I thanked the driver and followed her inside. She stalked straight to the elevator and tapped the call button repeatedly until it arrived. We reached our floor and Em went to her room without a word. I let her go. Tomorrow would be soon enough to talk.

CHAPTER

FORTY-TWO

I couldn't face dinner in the restaurant tonight. Didn't want to make small talk with Em and she likely wasn't in the mood either, so I ordered room service. While I waited for my food, I opened Em's ring binder.

Exorcisms, spells, prayers. Charms and cures. An interview with a woman who claimed to have been possessed and how she got rid of the demon. Em had highlighted a couple of the woman's comments in bright yellow, so I read through the article carefully. It seemed to be from the mid 1990s, but I figured exorcism techniques probably hadn't changed much.

As I reached the end of the interview, I noticed a small line of print right at the bottom of the page. It was so faint that I had to hold it up to the lamp to make it out. It was a name — an internet cafe maybe — and a date from September 2012.

I flicked through the next few pages before the significance of what I had seen hit me. I went back to the interview and checked the last line again. It definitely read September 2012. Did that mean Em had printed this page then? But why would she have been researching exorcism six years ago?

I thumbed through the rest of the printouts. Many were

undated, but I found others which seemed to have been printed in 2012 and early 2013. How strange. Perhaps Em had a particular interest in exorcisms. But why would she have brought the folder with her? Towards the end, I found a recipe that seemed to be some kind of potion to make oneself less attractive to demons. Beside it, in her small, neat handwriting, Em had written: *Tried 3 March 2013. No effect.*

I stared down at the words for a long time while my brain tried to make sense of them. Em had tried this potion five years ago. Had she been possessed herself? Then why didn't she say anything? Surely she would expect me to want to know that she had personal experience.

Unless she didn't want me to know. In my mind's eye, I saw her squeezing Jane Smith's hand before her appointment. Jane Smith had acquired the demon somewhere around 2010 if she had spoken the truth about having had it for eight years. Did Em know her? Had she been trying to help Jane Smith rid herself of the demon? Had she set up this entire tour just so that Jane Smith would have access to me? So she could pass on the demon to someone else who could hear it? Is that why she had insisted I continue with my individual consultations while on tour?

I grabbed the folder and went next door to Em's room. I knocked and from within heard her moving around.

"Em," I called. "Open up."

She cracked open the door and peered out at me.

"Now is not a good time, Dorothy."

"Jane Smith. Who is she?"

She paled a little and inhaled shakily.

"Whatever do you mean?" she asked.

"Why were you printing articles about demon possession back in 2012? Why is there a recipe with a comment that you tried it in 2013? Who is Jane Smith?"

"Dorothy, I realise you're under an enormous amount of stress—"

"Stop lying to me, Em. You engineered this whole thing, didn't you? You've known about Jane Smith all along. You've been trying to help her. I bet you could hardly believe your luck when you started working for me and realised you'd finally found someone else who could hear the spirits. What did you do? Did you ring her right away to say you'd found someone she could pass it on to?"

"It wasn't like that." She put her hands over her face for a moment, then opened the door wider. "You may as well come in. Let me explain."

I stormed into her room. It was impeccable. No rumpled bed or clothes spewing from the suitcase like in my room.

"Go on then," I said. "Tell me."

Em sighed. "Jess is my cousin. Her family lived just down the road from mine when we were kids and we were always close. They moved to America when she was fourteen."

"How lovely for you."

She ignored my sarcasm and continued.

"She used to tell me these stories about how she could talk to ghosts. It was all very thrilling while we were kids, but by the time her family moved away I had stopped believing her. I thought she was making it all up.

"We had a big argument about it a few weeks before she left. She insisted she wasn't lying and I insisted she had to be. We weren't on speaking terms by the time she left and we didn't have any contact for a few years after that. Then she rang me one day in a panic, talking about being possessed. I thought at first she must be on drugs, but as the days went on, she kept insisting.

"I had been wanting to travel to America and had half thought about contacting her. Seeing if we could reconcile, but I hadn't quite been able to make myself be the one to reach out. So I booked a flight and came over to see her."

She paced up and down the room now. I leaned against the closed door, clutching the ring binder to my chest.

"Go on," I said.

"As soon as I saw her, I could see it. The demon. It looked just the same as it does with you. Cloudy and insubstantial. I can't hear the spirits, as evidenced by the fact that it isn't the slightest bit interested in me, but I can see it. I can feel them sometimes too. The ones at your house. I've never seen them, but sometimes I go into a room and I can feel that someone else is there."

"Why didn't you tell me? I asked you if you could feel them."

She sighed again. "I didn't know how. I figured it would sound crazy. And I had promised Jess I would help her. That together we would get rid of the demon."

"You must have thought your lucky stars had aligned when you found out about my request for an assistant," I said, somewhat bitterly.

"I had no idea who you were. All the recruitment agency told me was that you ran a home-based consulting business. I fitted your requirements and they offered me the job."

"And then you arrived and realised I might just be the answer you were looking for."

"Not really." She looked me in the eye for the first time since she had opened the door. "Not at first. I assumed you were just another fake. Jess had been to every damn clairvoyant and medium and psychic she could find and they were all fakes. Why would I think you were any different? But after a couple of days, I started to think that maybe you were. I couldn't figure out how a fake could always know just the right thing to say to bring almost every client to tears. I often heard you talking to someone when I knew you were alone in the room. They left pretty quickly when I went in, but after a while I guess they knew I couldn't hear or see them and they started staying around. And I could feel them. I realised there was some kind of presence in the room and you were communicating with it."

"So you lined up this whole tour just so I could meet your cousin and she could hand her demon off to me?"

"No! It wasn't like that. I was just doing my job and doing it the best I could. You have a remarkable ability and I was trying to make the most of it for you. But I owe Jess my life. When we were ten years old, we were playing in the creek near our homes. I slipped on a rock and hit my head. Jess dragged me out of the water. I would have drowned if she hadn't been there, so I figured if I could help her with the demon, it would be no more than I owed her. I've dedicated all of my spare time for the last eight years to trying to find a solution for her."

So that must be the other commitments she had mentioned. It wasn't a child, after all.

"So why didn't I meet your cousin on the first trip? You could have invited her to the hotel, introduced us, made it all seem casual. Then she could have passed on the demon and been done with it."

"She was actually supposed to meet you on that trip, but she got the flu. She still tried to come, but they wouldn't let her on the plane since she was obviously unwell."

"How lucky for her that you managed to engineer a second trip then," I said.

"Dorothy, I didn't know that passing you the demon would block your connection with your spirit contacts. I didn't even realise you had specific contacts. I thought you were talking directly to the spirits your clients asked for."

"Your cousin never told you she suddenly couldn't hear other spirits anymore?"

"No, she didn't. I guess... I guess she assumed maybe the

demon scared them away or something. She never had any ability to summon them, although god knows she tried when we were kids. Maybe as she got older she didn't hear them as much anymore. I don't know. I've never thought to ask. You have to believe me that I never meant for any of this to happen."

"You just meant for your cousin to free herself of a demon by passing it onto me."

"Rick was not supposed to ask you to do a consultation. The producer promised me that wouldn't happen. But also, you didn't have to go along with it. You could have said no."

"So now it's my fault? You were the one who said I had to fake it or get sued. You said I had to keep going with the tour. All so you could cover your own behind after helping your cousin out. Well, guess what, Em, the tour's off. I'll leave you to handle the arrangements."

I opened the door, then turned back to her.

"And once you've done that, you can consider yourself fired."

FORTY-THREE

I managed to change my flight and book a seat home for the following evening. I spent the day in my hotel room with the door locked. Housekeeping came, but I sent them away. I switched off my mobile and didn't check messages or emails. Most people would contact Em anyway, but I didn't want to risk the possibility that anyone had my number. I had already missed at least two interviews. Would Em have contacted anyone to cancel or had she already gone, leaving me alone with the mess she had made?

It was hard not to blame her for everything, although I knew I shouldn't have gone along with it. If I had stood my ground back when she first tried to convince me to fake it, I would still have the demon, but I wouldn't have been exposed on national television. I could have continued with the tour, cancelling just the individual consultations. If I had refused Rick's surprise consultation, I would have left America with my reputation intact. As much as Em had manipulated the circumstances to her cousin's benefit, I only had myself to blame that everyone now thought I was a fake. That I had always been a fake.

My new flight wasn't until midnight and the day seemed to take forever, but finally I was on the plane and on my way home. I spent the fourteen-hour flight worrying about Gray and the others. Was he still able to see and hear me, even though I couldn't hear him? Maybe our channel of communication was blocked, but he was still there on the other side of the veil? Or maybe he had crossed over. Gone to wherever spirits are supposed to go. Maybe his disappearance had nothing to do with the demon. When I got home, the others might still be there.

I tried to stay hopeful through the long flight, but I knew it was unlikely that Gray had crossed over or just stopped talking to me. The demon was blocking my ability to hear him. I needed to find someone else who could hear it. Then it would leave me and I would be able to communicate with my spirit friends again. Maybe I could restore my reputation. Tell people what had happened. Explain I had made a mistake in trying to fake it.

The demon was still and quiet on the flight. It stirred at one point, just a slight readjustment of its position, but then settled and seemed to go back to sleep or whatever it did. Its presence made me think about Michael Bright, the lightbulb-shattering spirit that had arrived with Ms Hathson. That must have been four or five months ago. In all that time, I had rarely encountered any unpleasant spirits and that was the only time I had felt threatened.

Perhaps I should have taken the knowledge that dangerous spirits existed more seriously. Bec and Lissa's newfound, and possibly temporary, abilities were another warning. Maybe if I had been less casual about these signs, I would have reacted faster when I realised there was something wrong with Jane Smith. I already had all the information I needed to know that not all spirits were friendly. That some might be dangerous. But I had been complacent. I had let my trust in my spirit friends convince me that there was little possibility of harm to myself.

We landed in Brisbane at seven a.m. The plane sat on the tarmac for half an hour before we were allowed to disembark and I was almost ready to scream with frustration by the time the doors opened. Several flights had landed and it took more than an hour to get through Immigration. I didn't let myself look for Em. Perhaps she was on my flight, perhaps she wasn't. It made no difference to me.

I had left LA in summer and it was winter when I arrived home. Not that winter means cold in Brisbane. The morning air was chilly enough that I wished I had thought to leave my jacket out of my suitcase, but the day would warm up soon enough.

As the taxi turned down my street, my pulse pounded. Would I be able to hear my spirit friends? Maybe I'd be able to speak to the others, even if I still couldn't hear Gray himself. Maybe they would tell me he was there, that nothing had happened to him. That I just couldn't hear him anymore. Maybe he was now tied to the house instead of me and couldn't reach me in LA. The demon was restless, sliding around my neck and repositioning itself. Perhaps it sensed my distress.

The house looked the same as when I left. Paint peeled from the front steps — I had been meaning to do something about that for months — and a few leaves poked over the edges of the gutters. Someone had mowed the grass while I was away. Em must have arranged for a gardener to visit.

I took a deep breath and inserted my key in the front door. The key stuck and I caught myself thinking that I'd have to tell Em to get a locksmith in. Then I remembered I had fired her. The house smelled stuffy, just like one would expect for a house that had been closed up for weeks. I could immediately feel that I was alone. Still, I called for them anyway.

"I'm home. Are you guys here? Gray?"

Silence. Nothing but my own voice echoing through the rooms.

"Bec? Lissa? Samson?"

I waited, but they didn't answer. It didn't necessarily mean there was a problem. They might just be somewhere else, busy with something. But no matter how many times I called, they never answered. I never felt them arrive, either. If they were still there, I could neither hear nor feel them.

Dinner that night was a sad affair of a microwaved meal in front of the television. The house was quiet and felt emptier than ever before. I went to bed early. The flight and the long days of interviews had exhausted me, not to mention the sleepless nights spent trying to contact Gray. Once I was rested, I would be able to think more clearly. I would come up with a plan. As I tossed and turned, the demon shifted around my neck, reminding me I wasn't as alone as I felt.

FORTY-FOUR

As darkness fell one evening towards the end of winter, I opened a bottle of wine and sat on my cracked leather couch. I had moved it back into the lounge room and set it in front of the television where it used to sit. The wing-back chairs were back in the spare room. I couldn't bear to look at them. They were a reminder of a time that was passed.

"Well, that's another day finished."

I didn't know whether they could hear me, but I talked to them every day. I wanted them to know that I hadn't forgotten them. That someone remembered.

A reporter had arrived on my doorstep today and asked to interview me. I closed the door in his face.

"I never wanted fame or celebrity. You guys know that, better than anyone. Right back at the start, the only thing I wanted was to find a way to keep my house. Remember how you had to talk me into offering consultations? If I hadn't been so desperate for the money, I wouldn't have done it. But I figured that if I could keep the house and maybe help some people along the way, it would be a good thing."

I took a couple of sips of my wine while I pondered what else I wanted to tell them.

"But I let it get too big. I got too big. The tours, the television interviews, the talk shows. I never wanted any of it. You know that. But I forgot why I was doing it. I let myself get swept away and forgot it was supposed to be about helping people."

I turned on the television, flicked through a few channels. Muted it but left it on. The flickering light made me feel a little less lonely. Without the television, the only noise was the sound of the traffic outside. Cars sped past, truck brakes groaned, a horn beeped. The peak hour traffic would settle over the next hour, but for now, at least there was noise in the house.

I had almost got used to the demon's constant presence. It felt kind of like a warm scarf, tightly wrapped around my neck. Sometimes it would stir, give me a brief squeeze as if to remind me that if it wanted to, it could choke the breath out of me. But then it would go back to sleep or whatever it did. I tried speaking to it many times, but it never spoke to me again. I wondered whether I imagined that one time I thought I heard it.

"I miss you, guys. I'm still looking for a way to get rid of the demon. I spend every day on my research and I'm booking consultations with every speaker I can find. There's got to be someone else like me out there. Someone who can hear. I just need to find them. Once I pass the demon on to the next person, we will be able to talk again."

I never let myself think too hard about the ethics of passing the demon on. If it wasn't for Gray and the others, I wouldn't even try. I would do what Jane Smith, or Jess as Em called her, had intended to do: keep it until I died and hope that my death somehow sucked it out of the mortal plane. But I couldn't live the rest of my life knowing I would never again speak with Gray, Bec, Lissa and Samson.

I had finally done an internet search on my address and was unsurprised to find the house had not always been a happy home. Bec had died here, in a fall down the stairs in the middle of the night. Years earlier, Lissa's family had lived here, although they moved away soon after her death. I had been right when I thought Lissa was murdered, although it hadn't happened in the house. A man who lived a few houses down was arrested for her murder and found guilty. He died in prison without ever ceasing to insist on his innocence. His name was Samson.

Gray was the only one I couldn't find anything about. It made me more certain that he must be my brother. Something he had said the day I visited Mona had stuck with me, although it was only recently that I had realised why. *You had better say something, Dorothy. I'm just gagging for it.* Gary had said something like that to me once. *I'm just gagging for it.* I couldn't remember the details of that conversation, no matter how hard I tried. But the phrase stuck with me. What I couldn't explain was why his voice didn't sound like Gary, but I supposed there was a lot I didn't know about what had happened to him. Maybe it wasn't unusual for a spirit to sound different from how they had in life. Maybe the more traumatic the death, the more they were changed.

Did Gray himself know? From his odd reaction the couple of times we had spoken about it, I thought he did, or he at least suspected. I just didn't know why he hadn't told me. Maybe he didn't want me to know he was stuck on the other side of the veil.

It must be an awful, tedious existence. An eternity of waiting, of watching the people you loved grow old and die. And then what? What happened to the spirit once there was nobody they loved left alive? Was this what happened to all of us? Did we all just hang around on the other side of the veil, waiting and watching? There had to be more to the afterlife than that. What was the point of living if that was all it led to?

And what of the demon? Had it originally been a living person? What had happened to cause it to become what it had, rather than being like my spirit friends? Maybe it had never been human. Maybe it was something else altogether.

I hadn't told the spirits what I had learned about them. I had broken their rules, of course, but I figured that didn't matter anymore. If they were watching me still, they already knew anyway.

"Gray, I need to tell you something," I said. "And I hope you can hear me. I want you to know how sorry I am that I didn't answer the phone that day. I'm sorry I never rang you back. Sorry I was such a terrible sister. And I'm sorry that because of these unresolved issues between us, you're stuck in my house. I wish there was something I could do. When I get rid of this demon and we can talk again, that's what I'll work on. I'll find a way for you to go wherever you're supposed to move on to. I promise you, I will be a much better sister from now on."

CHAPTER

FORTY-FIVE

As lights were switched off and the living inhabitant went to bed, the house settled in for the night. There were a few creaks and groans as it adjusted. At length, all was quiet.

The spirits roamed the house, silent and invisible to all but each other. There was an addition to their number now, one with whom the house was familiar, for she had visited many times. She had formed a bond with the house, whether she knew it or not. So it was natural that after her death, this was where she would return to.

The others were unsurprised when she arrived. If anyone was going to join them on the other side of the veil, they had always known it would be her. With time, they adjusted, and where there used to be four, now there were five.

Enjoyed this book? I'd love for you to leave a short review on the retailer you purchased from.

For bookclub discussion questions, see https://kyliequillinan.com/bookclubs/

ALSO BY KYLIE QUILLINAN

The Amarna Age Series

Book One: *Queen of Egypt*

Book Two: *Son of the Hittites*

Book Three: *Eye of Horus*

Book Four: *Gates of Anubis*

Book Five: *Lady of the Two Lands*

Book Six: *Guardian of the Underworld*

Daughter of the Sun: An Amarna Age Novella

The Amarna Princesses Series

Book One: *Outcast*

Book Two: *Catalyst*

Book Three: *Warrior*

Palace of the Ornaments Series

Book One: *Princess of Babylon*

Book Two: *Ornament of Pharaoh*

Book Three: *Child of the Alliance*

Book Four: *A Game of Senet*

Book Five: *Secrets of Pharaoh*

Book Six: *Hawk of the West*

See kyliequillinan.com for more books, including exclusive collections, and newsletter sign up.

ABOUT THE AUTHOR

Kylie writes about women who defy society's expectations. Her novels are for readers who like fantasy with a basis in history or mythology. Her interests include Dr Who, jellyfish and cocktails. She needs to get fit before the zombies come.

Swan – the epilogue to the Tales of Silver Downs series – is available exclusively to her newsletter subscribers. Sign up at kyliequillinan.com.

www.ingramcontent.com/pod-product-compliance
Lightning Source LLC
Chambersburg PA
CBHW030618120726
47904CB00006B/1952